THE CURSE OF ANUBIS

By: T. David Sergent

TABLE OF CONTENT

CHAPTER 1

EGYPT 2000 BC

The screaming was constant and came from different directions and always ended with a snarl or a choking, gurgling sound that did nothing to calm the frightened family. The small hut was their only refuge as they stared over the table at the simple wooden shutters, the only thing separating them from whatever was outside. The woman held a baby to her breast trying to keep it silent. The father had one hand on his wife's arm and the other on a leg of the table that he had broken off. Ointment ran down his face making his eyes sting. He had, at one point, run an arm across his face smearing it further down his cheek.

"We must pray to Isis and Osiris as they too know the love of a child and will help us," the woman whispered, looking up at her husband with tears in her desperate eyes. He looked back down at her and tried to smile reassuringly.

The baby stopped suckling then and began to cry, full now from his mother's milk and sensing their tension. She tried to bounce him soothingly in her arms, but the baby was picking up momentum.

They snapped their heads up as they heard scraping on the shutters that was immediately followed by what sounded like a twice intake of breath. It was only a small meager latch that kept whatever it was from coming inside.

"Re's might protect us," the woman whispered, bouncing the child desperately. They watched as something outside pushed the shutters which bent inward, with the latch threatening to break off. The father looked down at his small family and gently touched his wife's face. She looked up at him, wide-eyed. The ointment on her delicate Egyptian features made trails down her face from the tears. The baby wailed and she shook her head apologetically under his gaze.

"It's alright," he said stroking her cheek. "No matter what happens … know that we three will always be together. Osiris shall welcome us and see our hearts are light when measured, and that our Kas are full of love for our gods, our family, and for Egypt."

The shutters smashed to pieces, leaving only thick darkness beyond. The man stood, table leg firmly in his hand. The baby was quiet now, surprised by the noise. The man stepped around the table, gathering his courage. His wife reached out to him, but he was already committed and moved forward. He walked up to the window, head low and ready to spring back if needed. He could smell the blood and he instinctively tried to cover his nose with his arm. He sensed movement outside below the window and leaned out, swinging down with the table leg, jumping back as soon as his arm finished its descent.

The mother cradled the now-silent, curious baby as she peered around the table. She watched her husband creep slowly to the window, stepping over the broken pieces of the shutter. As she watched, she thought her heart would leap from her chest. She covered her mouth as he leaned slowly out of the opening. A dark shape sprang up from under

2

the window, pulling him into the darkness as he screamed. She watched breathlessly as he was pulled into the darkness. She stood, stepping forward, reaching out her hand, not knowing what to do. She heard a ripping, then his gurgling … a crunch … and then silence. All that was left was the distant horrified yelling further away into the darkness.

"No," she whispered, her hand still reaching forward. As if in answer, the small amount of light that had come into the window as her beloved disappeared went dark again. She watched as the darkness climbed through the open window and into the room. She heard an intake of breath in front of her and sensed, more than saw, something rise above her. She held very still, grateful the baby was still not crying. Something snapped down near her; she felt the air move close to her face and as she opened her eyes, she was looking into the golden eyes of a monster. She was too frightened to move. The baby sensed its mother's fear and began to whimper.

The front door of the hut suddenly burst apart and something large slid across the floor towards her. The dark thing in front of her turned towards it and she was able to tear her gaze away, like waking from some type of spell. She saw that the creature that had crashed onto the floor was struggling to get up. When it did, she found herself staring up into the eyes of yet another dark monster. It stood like a man on two legs but hunched over like an animal. Its jaws protruded from its face as it sneered wickedly down at her. More light came from the new hole where there used to be a door. A long red tongue came out, licking its jowls hungrily as it lowered itself to spring at her. She closed her eyes and held her baby tightly to her chest. The room was filled with a howling rage and then she heard a crash. When she realized that she was still alive, she opened her eyes and saw that both creatures were now gone. She looked around, confused, finding a hole in the wall next to her. She heard fighting beyond. A large snarling head came through the hole near the floor, looking up at her. She jumped away as it was pulled back into the hole with claws scraping the floor as it tried to get to her.

She turned and ran to the open space where the door once was as fast as her sandaled feet would carry her, clutching her crying baby to her chest as she ran outside. She screamed for help, running into the dirt-packed road, but stopped as she found many other villagers screaming for help. Everywhere she looked, her neighbors were being run down by the big dark shapes of the creatures. The creatures ripped into them as they screamed, struggled, and begged for help. She could only watch, taking in the massacre, one after another, and not knowing which way to run.

"Oh, great Anpu, why? Why do you judge us so?" She looked up to the dark sky. "Re help us! HELP US!" she yelled at the empty night sky. The screams were suddenly broken by the sharp, crisp sound of a horn. It even made the dying look in the direction it came from. She followed the sound with hope now in her heart. She saw the creatures look up from their killing and into the sky, their heads turned sideways in a strange, canine way. She followed their gaze up into the darkness and heard the faint whistling sound that she thought could only be Re's *sickle* rushing through the air to strike down Anpu's cruelty upon his people.

She fell to the ground in reverence, reaching to the sky with one arm as she clutched her baby to her breast. As tears of gratitude rolled

4

down her cheeks, arrows came out of the darkness and thudded into her again and again, killing her and pinning her baby to her chest. She fell to the ground with a smile of gratitude still on her lips; the arrows protruding from her chest following her still outstretched hand towards the heavens.

The beasts in the streets fell to the ground, withering in pain, as they desperately pulled at the arrows that kept falling like rain. Everyone on the street fell to the ground, dead or dying. The ones that were in the deeper darkness of the village, either eating or being eaten, ran or crawled for shelter. Two more quick, sharp blasts of the horn and soldiers ran in shooting more arrows and stabbing with swords everything that moved. Some of the beasts fought but were quickly overwhelmed. Blood from both beast and man ran into the streets like the flooding of the Nile. No man, woman, or child was spared.

Meanwhile, a man on a horse slowly rode into the small town. His head was shaved, and he wore a flowing red robe that was traditional for a priest of his standing. He stopped and watched the carnage unfolding before him with cold, detached eyes. He heard movement off to his left and looked lazily over as one of the beasts sprang at him, snarling. It did not even make it completely off the ground before a foray of arrows from behind the man sent it to the ground.

The priest watched it twitch as it passed into the underworld where it would be judged.

"Vile thing," he muttered. He leaned forward in his saddle with one arm and concentrated on the battle in front of him. He watched silently for a few moments before looking over to his right and making eye contact with a soldier who waited there patiently with a horn strapped around his neck. The priest nodded to him.

The man hesitated. "Are you sure, holy one?" he asked nervously.

The priest stared down at him with fire in his eyes. "It must stop here, he said, tightening his grip on the saddle. "Do as you are commanded or Anpu's jackals will be the least of your problems." The soldier took a step back from the priest before bowing submissively.

"As you command, benevolent one," the soldier said quickly, and put the horn to his lips. He blew two long, sorrowful notes. The priest did not appreciate the added touch and scowled at the soldier who looked to the ground, sadly.

Barrels of oil were ignited, and soldiers behind the priest lit their arrows and let them fly. The soldiers and beasts that were still alive stopped and looked at the sky as it lit up in flames. Some of the soldiers who recognized what the flames above them meant turned an angry eye on the single man on horseback as he watched them from up the road. The arrows hit everything including the grass roofs which instantly went up in flames. More arrows followed like fiery waves against the Nile's dark shores. The priest watched as the town went up in flames and listened silently to the unanswered cries. He reached beneath his robe with his free arm and pulled out a small dark statue.

It was the figure of a god that had the body of a man with a head of a jackal. "I hope you judge these poor bastards better in death then you did in life, Anpu," the priest said bitterly before throwing the statuette to the ground. As he did, he noticed his bandaged arm and stared at it, frowning. The white linen was stained with blood and pus. But that was not what the priest's eyes went to or what made his heart go cold. Beyond the fold of the bandages, blackness crept up his arm. He stared at it for a moment more before looking around to see if anyone had seen him, then he hid the arm once more beneath his robe. The battle-hardened horse under him sensed something it did not like and shifted uneasily.

CHAPTER 2
PRESENT DAY

It was no use pretending any longer that he didn't have to go. The blankets may have been keeping out the light, but his body would not forget that he had been sleeping for more than twelve hours. Jack pushed himself up to the corner of the bed, holding his head in his hands and trying to keep the room from spinning. It was no use; he knew he had gone too far into the deep end to have it stop hurting now.

His mouth felt like he had been eating cat litter. He knew that just outside the door to his room there was a toilet and possibly some kind of liquid in the fridge. The only problem was the looming bright light that was coming from under the door. It was as if it was saying, 'Sooner or later you will have to open that door and then I will have you!' He stood slowly and looked for something to hide the light from his eyes. On the dresser, among the half-empty beer cans and cigarette butts, was a hat his mother had bought him as a joke from Disney World.

She had gone a few months ago with her new boyfriend and sent him this as a gift. It was an oversized baseball hat with long Goofy ears hanging off the sides, but he didn't care what it looked like, so he put it on and lowered the visor to his eyebrows. He found his red robe on the floor and put it over his boxers and beer-stained 'wifebeater' tank top.

He had to admit the Goofy hat did feel comfortable on his aching head. It was almost as if the hat was just tight enough to keep his tortured brain from spilling out onto the dirty and sticky wooden floor of their rented apartment. He opened the door leading to the hallway like a soldier bravely ready to walk into the line of fire. His plan was simple. Open the door with his Goofy hat rim low and move stealthily to the bathroom, which was only maybe three or four paces away at most. With luck, the shades were still drawn there.

He threw open the door and the late afternoon daylight hit him like a hammer falling on a gnat. He stepped back with thoughts of retreat but knew the end would justify the means … and that he would piss his pants if he did not go soon. So, he walked quickly until reaching the bathroom door. He reached for the handle, already knowing his plan had been flawed from the beginning. His Goofy hat had been too low to see that the bathroom door was closed and someone else was using it. He could hear the shower running. Thankfully, he remembered that a few weeks back he and another roommate had to force open the door to help Marty who had, in a drunken state, fallen asleep on the toilet again. He knew he only had to lift the door slightly and push and it would open. He did and moved quickly, with success only inches away. He barely had the seat lifted before relieving himself with a sigh of relief.

"Sorry, man," he said to the running shower.

"You prick!" answered a feminine voice from behind the curtain. "Get the fuck out of here!"

"Oh. Sorry, Michelle," Jack said, noticing that even the sound of Marty's girlfriend's name made the taste in his mouth go from cat litter to dog shit.

Michelle had been living there for several months now. How many nobody really knew. To him she was like the mildew that grew around the tub. No telling when it first got there, but now it was taking over everything. Jack hawked up a good size ball of snot and spat it into the toilet.

"Are you hard of..."

"When you start paying some of the rent then you can talk shit," Jack answered under his breath but loud enough for her to hear. He flushed the toilet and hurried out before she could really lay into him. When he closed the door, he heard the satisfying screams from the shower. It was an old building and warm water seemed to vanish with every drop used elsewhere. Flush a toilet and ... well.

He knew everyone else would be at class right now, so other than the human mildew known as Michelle, everything should be quiet. He opened the refrigerator and was overpowered by the smell. It bent him over as he went into dry heaves. It was spring and the remains of Christmas turkey sat rotting inside. Slamming the door shut, he came face to face with a note on a magnet in his own writing. It said: Don't forget to meet with Dr. Usher at 1:00 pm on Thursday. DON'T FORGET!

A cold chill ran through him as he concentrated on what day it was. It was Thursday.

Shit!

He lifted his Goofy hat and looked at the kitchen clock. It said 2:30 pm. Another chill gripped Jack's heart. The message on the answering machine from Dr. Usher on Tuesday had said. "...this is your last chance. Don't be late!"

Shit, shit, and SHIT!

He ran into his room and threw off his robe and boxers. He found some jeans and a t-shirt on the floor and pulled them on, still swearing. Heading for the door, he grabbed his backpack of books that he had never even opened and swung them over his shoulder as a prop for his meeting.

"You going like that?" Michelle said with a towel around her and her dark wet hair hanging behind her. Jack turned back to her and had a thought that he just attributed to the alcohol from last night. Damn, she looked good. If it were not for her attitude, she would even be attractive.

"That hat is stupid," she said, leaning against the wall and crossing her arms. Her look was so smug that suddenly she was just the freeloading Michelle again. He had something really good to yell back when he remembered the Goofy hat. He reached up and felt the long ears falling down his head. He pulled it off and ran back for a replacement. Then he left without saying a word.

"You're welcome!" Michelle yelled after him.

Bitch.

The school was about a mile or so from where they lived, so it would actually take more time to take the car and find a parking spot ... so he ran. Just about halfway down the affluent road with its grandiose Victorian houses, he stopped and threw up in some primly trimmed bushes. When he was able to stand again, he saw an old man holding a running hose in his hand. He was standing in his yard staring at him with his mouth open in disbelief. Jack nodded apologetically and pulled his hat low before jogging on towards the school.

At the campus, he was feeling better but wished he had some gum or anything to get the taste of vomit out of his mouth. Instead of going straight to the faculty building, he decided to get something from the vending machine in the building next to it. As late as he was, he didn't figure it would make a difference now if he stopped for a soda and some gum. He entered the building and headed for the vending machines, feeling as if someone was watching him. There were people walking everywhere, it was a college campus after all.

At the top of the stairs, he saw a vending machine that looked as if someone had recently beaten the crap out of it. The Coke symbol on the front had duct tape holding it together and the light was blinking as if at any minute the life of that machine was going to be out forever. He reached into his pocket for change and realized he had forgotten his wallet in his haste to get here. He swore, wanting to punish the machine more when he heard someone nervously clearing their throat from behind him.

He turned, surprised, and looked down at a short girl with a close-cropped haircut and suspenders.

"Excuse me," she said, adjusting her backpack nervously and smiling widely to expose the braces on her still-crooked teeth. "Are you … well -- I mean … ah," she stammered nervously.

"Are you in the School of Archaeology?" he asked, knowing where this was going but having no patience for the girl's obvious shyness. He needed to go meet with Dr. Usher.

"Yes," she stammered. "And I am a very big fan of your father, Dr. Edwards."

"I see," Jack answered with mock politeness, all while looking longingly at the stairs. He hadn't been to class in months and as soon as he walked into the building people were already telling him how wonderful his father was.

"I have read everything he has ever published," she said, looking up at him with an undying admiration in her eyes that Jack knew wasn't for him.

"He would have been so proud," he said, smiling politely and turning.

"Wait," she said, reaching out a hand. Jack stopped, sighing, and looked back. "I just wanted to say, as she brushed her hair from her eyes nervously. "I just want to say that he was a great man. And that I'm sorry for your loss." Past the braces and the bulky suspenders, he decided the girl was pretty, in a frumpy kind of way. Jack could have seen his father offering her an internship ... as he would so often to girls just like her.

"Thanks," he said again, springing to the glass doors before the fanatical girl stopped him again. He felt her eyes on him all the way to the door and part of the way to the faculty building. He could almost hear

13

her thoughts. 'Such a waste ... a genius like Dr. Edwards spawning a loser like him.'

God I hate this school. He thought as he moodily pushed open the doors that led to the faculty building.

But as much as he hated the school, he knew it was his father's name that had gotten him in. It had a large archaeological program and his father ... when he was not on a dig, which he almost always was, was once part of it. He also knew that a good part of that program was supported by grants from Dr. Edwards.

He wondered if they knew how the great Dr. Edwards got his money. And if they did, would that have even put a ding in his father's gleaming silver armor? A dull pounding started in his head as he came to stand before Dr. Usher's office. There were others in the hall sitting on the floor, waiting. He would not have been surprised if some of the nerdy ones were just sitting around because they had nowhere else to go. Archaeology always seemed to attract the freaks.

"Excuse me," one of the boys said, standing with that same look in his eyes the girl had. "Are you-" but, before he could finish, Jack opened the door to Dr. Usher's office and stepped inside, closing the door behind him with a bang.

Geeks and freaks, he thought, shaking his head.

When he turned, he saw Dr. Usher sitting at his desk, looking at him red-faced and strangely uncomfortable.

"I am *so* sorry…" Jack started, spreading his hands wide. That was when he saw a tall dark man standing in the shadows of the room.

"Come in, Jack," Dr. Usher said, pointing to a chair with a forced smile on his fat lips. Dr. Usher was one of those archaeological professors that had never spent time in the field. He had always been friendly with Jack's father, but Jack never missed the jealous looks Dr. Usher would shoot his father behind his back. The short, plump man with about three hairs on head found great pleasure now seeing Dr. John Edwards' only son struggling through his classes.

He knew the man hated him because of his father, but just like the many that loved him because of his father, he really did not give a shit.

"And what was it that kept me waiting in my office all afternoon for you?" Dr. Usher asked, leaning back into his chair, frowning and crossing his chubby arms. Jack was still looking at the man standing by the curtains quietly watching them. Dr. Usher cleared his throat, annoyed, and Jack looked back at him.

"Sorry … what?"

"Listen to me you little piece of-, Dr. Usher started, but the mysterious man in the shadows of the room stepped forward and, without saying a word, commanded both their attention. He was wearing a dark suit and a red hat with the insignia of the college. He had dark skin and an impossibly long nose. His hands were crossed behind him as he stared coldly at Jack.

"Please excuse my intrusion," he said in what Jack recognized as a thick Middle Eastern accent. "But I am in need of the skills that I hope run in your family." Jack was no stranger to the ways of Middle Eastern men. Growing up, his father had many *friends* coming and going from the house.

"I am not my father," Jack said, returning the cold stare but feeling more like the prey of a swooping falcon than a defiant son.

"Yes, yes of course you are not," the man said, extending his hand and walking forward with a smile that did not reach his eyes. "I have been rude. Please beg your pardon, Mr. Edwards. I am Raul Gonzalez."

He was Raul Gonzalez like Jack was the Pope, he thought, standing and taking the man's hand. 'Raul' squeezed it and did not let go.

"You have your father's face, but not his grip," he said, finally letting go. Jack felt his face turning red and turned for the door. "If you leave through that door, you are abandoning any chance of graduating from this school, young man," Dr. Usher shot after him angrily. Jack paused and sighed again before turning back to the chubby man behind the desk.

Dr. Usher smiled smugly as Jack turned towards him. "I do not care whose son you are. I will not allow you to make a mockery of this department, not to mention this school." Jack knew that if it were not for his father, no one would have even heard of this crappy school. He thought it but didn't dare say it.

"I have a proposition to offer you, Mr. Edwards," Raul said smiling.

"It's Jack," Jack said, looking back to the man in the suit and ridiculous hat.

"Jack, then," Raul said, smiling wider as if he was the only one to know some secret joke. "I would like you to finish the expedition your father had..." Raul took a breath as if finding the words, but Jack knew 'failed' was what he was about to say.

"...unfinished."

Jack did not miss the quick smile that flashed across Dr. Usher's face. He wanted to pick the man's stapler off his desk and throw it at his fat bald head. The man was a fat little wanna-be archaeologist who must have died every time his father made a find.

"I am not an archaeologist ... Raul."

"I'll say," Dr. Usher put in, laughing bitterly. Jack continued as if he had never heard the jibe. "My father had his life, and I am now living mine," he said, feeling a bout of nausea and lightheadedness coming.

"Do you plan to spend your life drinking and smoking away what your father worked for?" Raul asked, crossing his arms once again behind him in a way that reminded Jack of some Nazi soldier from the old movies he and Marty watched as kids.

"What I plan to do with my life is none of your concern, *Mr. Gonzalez*. And what do you know of it anyway?" he asked, getting angry.

"I know very much of it, Jack," the man said frowning and taking a step forward, making Jack take one backwards. "I know you are failing out of this school. I know that you spend all your time drinking and smoking that poison grass in that small dirty apartment of yours." Raul brought his face close to Jack's now. "And I know that you are wasting your life, but that is going to change, yes?"

"How's that, Raul?" Jack asked, trying to sound brave.

"You are going to Egypt to succeed where your father failed. You are going to bring me the scroll of Anubis, and you are leaving the day after tomorrow." Raul smiled underneath his baseball hat like a cat before biting off the head of a mouse.

"Egypt? No way am I going to Egypt!" Jack said laughing. "What about my classes?" he asked, turning to Dr. Usher who rolled his eyes at him disgustedly.

"You have not stepped one foot into any of your classes in months," Dr. Usher said, shaking his head. "You are going to Egypt, or you are failing and that is that."

"Why me? Just because my father is who he is?" Raul pulled a pack of Marlboro Reds from his pocket and lit a cigarette. Jack could see that Dr. Usher was on the verge of objecting but restrained himself. *What does this man have over chubby Usher?* Jack couldn't help thinking.

"Yes," Raul said, puffing out a cloud of smoke and pulling aside the thick curtains to peak outside. "We have chosen you because you are Dr. John Edwards' son. I would think that was obvious. Why else would we be having this conversation?"

"Because you recognize the skills?" Jack asked, smiling sarcastically. Raul looked back with a raised eyebrow, but a smile was nowhere on his face. "Start packing. And do not..."

"Fail?" Jack finished for him.

Raul looked back to the window, shaking his head.

"If I do find the scroll thing does that mean I graduate?" Jack asked boldly of Dr. Usher. The man's face turned an impossible shade of purple.

"Yes," Raul answered for him.

"I will need Marty too ... to help with the research."

"The drug dealer? No way!" Dr. Usher shouted, furiously getting up from his desk. "You may take whom you like ... that is reasonable," Raul said absently without even acknowledging Usher.

"That means he graduates as well?" Jack thought the whole strange meeting so far was worth the look on Dr. Usher's face.

"Spare me any more details, Mr. Edwards," Raul said, throwing down his cigarette and crushing it on Dr. Usher's rug. "The good doctor here will work out the rest. A team has already been put together to help you find the Anubis scroll. Take who and what you need to make this successful." With that, he took two quick steps to the door and opened it, pausing. He turned his cold dark eyes on Jack once more. "You will be on that plane." It was not a question.

"Don't I get to think about it?" Jack asked, sincerely nervous now.

"No," Raul Gonzalez said, and quietly closed the door behind him.

Dr. Usher sat back down in his chair and frowned deeply. Jack was unsure if it was from the stranger leaving or his discontent with his presence. "Be at this address the day after tomorrow at nine a.m. Be packed and ready with anyone you want to bring. No excuses and no problems," he said, rubbing his temples.

"Who is that guy?" Jack asked him.

Dr. Usher took a moment before answering. "He is an important investor in this school and more specifically in this department."

"I do not recall a 'Raul Gonzalez' building on campus?"

"Get out of my office," Dr. Usher said, without looking up.

"What about plane tickets?" Jack asked, spreading his hands, confused. "I think I need to renew my passport too."

"…that all will be taken care of. Just arrive at that address at nine. Not ten or eleven … nine … A.M. Don't screw this up and get the *fuck* out of my office … NOW!"

CHAPTER 3
JUMPING IN

It was 8:30 a.m. and Jack and Marty were throwing things into as many bags as they had. They had to use garbage bags for the things that did not fit in the luggage. Marty kept shaking his head and stopping to take long drags on what they called their house bong, which was a tube that made long gurgling sounds when sucking smoke from it.

Marty let out a big cloud of smoke and smiled with his squinty eyes. Jack looked and laughed, shaking his head. Marty had been a constant friend since grade school. He was smart, but had chosen a lifestyle that revolved around marijuana. That's not to say he did poorly in school. In fact, Marty was an exceptional student and a voracious reader. Problem was that he was not the image of a 'good student,' so professors of the school tried to blackball him any chance they could. But Marty always seemed to bounce back. And it didn't hurt being best friends with the son of one of the most famous archaeologists that ever lived at a school that prided itself on its archaeology school.

Marty shook his head, bouncing his blond white-boy dreadlocks. He wore a beat-up Mexican poncho, faded jeans, and old sandals that barely looked like they could last another day.

"Dude, we got to go," Jack said, hauling his stuff to the front door.

"How long 'til we get there again?" Marty asked, packing more grass into his plastic tie-dye bong.

"Mapquest says 45 minutes and its 8:35 now."

"That don't work," Marty said, trying to hold his breath.

"Dude. LET'S GO!" Jack yelled at him.

Marty made a mock face of wonderment at Jack's reaction. "You didn't even want to go, man. Have a change of heart?" Marty asked in a throaty voice.

"Yeah, this will make it possible that I can graduate. And that, my fried little friend, means my trust fund doubles." Jack smiled at the thought. "That could mean a house in South Beach. Tits and ass every day ... and night." Jack bounced his brow mischievously.

"So, what the hell are we waiting for, man?" Marty smiled back merrily and swayed a bit.

Jack drove Marty's little Toyota pickup, weaving in and out of traffic. Their luggage slid from side to side in the truck bed, banging loudly. Marty was blowing hits out the window and bopping his head to a Grateful Dead bootleg on the MP3 player wired to the car radio.

"This music sucks," Jack said, looking sideways at his friend, disgusted.

"It's the music of the people. And you think it sucks?" Marty breathed in a big hit from his pipe. "- ... hen it sucks the poison from our souls, man." Seconds later, he let out a big cloud of smoke through his smiling teeth as if he were a dragon.

"No, I mean it sucks shit. It's the same fucking song over and over. These guys…"

"Are geniuses," Marty finished for him, his head moving up and down to the beat. "In their time, did people get Van Gogh? Or Beethoven? Or the comedy of Lenny Bruce? All pioneers in their field, man. All changed the world in their own way. With their own style, man. Same as The Grateful Dead." They both grabbed for a handhold as the tires screeched around a sharp corner.

"Bunch of shit," Jack said, re-adjusting into his seat. "Just because something sucks doesn't mean it's some genius creation only to be understood by the stoned of their generation."

"The Grateful Dead have been idolized in their generation and continue to inspire today, dude," Marty countered defensively.

"Yeah, well. People have also idolized Flock of Seagulls and Duran Duran … that don't make them good."

"Are you kidding?" Marty asked, flicking his lighter and lighting his pipe. "The Flock of Seagulls fuck'n rule, dude!" he said in a sucking voice with raised eyebrows.

"You smoked yourself stupid, asshole," Jack said, laughing and shaking his head.

"Whatever," Marty answered, blowing the smoke onto the dashboard and watching the patterns it made. "Hey, shouldn't we talk about the scroll thingy or something?" Jack shrugged in response. "Well,

23

I mean, we are about to meet somebody I never met before and be whisked off to Egypt for crap's sake!"

"Whisked? Dude, you're gay," Jack said laughing. "Who the hell says 'whisked'?"

"Dude, really. What the fuck do we do if we can't find the Anubis Scroll thing? What do we do then?" Marty asked, trying to sound serious.

"Then we stuff our pockets with artifacts like my oh-so-noble father did and make our own fortune. It's a win-win, dude." Marty looked over but didn't say anything at first.

"Your dad ripped off archaeological sites? Dude, that can't be true ... no way." Jack started laughing bitterly. "Did you think the grave robbing business was about true altruism and the great American way or some shit?"

Marty just stared at him. "Well Mr. 200 IQ, let me ask you this." Jack went on honking the horn and swearing at an old man he passed on the shoulder.

"Do you think that a dusty textbook on Archaeological Practices and Modern Techniques for the Most Successful Digs by Dr. Jonathan Edwards could buy a house in Beverly Hills and all the other shit our family has? Come on, man? You still with me here?" Jack said, pointing two fingers to his eyes. Marty knew talking about Jack's father was a touchy subject and said nothing. "The man is worshipped as if he was a conquering hero of Egyptian culture but all the while he stole the country blind. Oh, sure most of the big pieces made it to the Cairo Museum or

24

some other dull existence behind three inches of glass somewhere … but not all of it." Jack looked at the printout of directions lying between his legs and turned onto another quiet road. "How much do you think one golden ring with the symbol of the great Pharaoh O-tut-who-gives-a-shit would be worth on the open market?"

"A shit load," Marty answered.

"Yeah, now times that by 30 years of digging in that hot scratchy shit finding one after another."

"But he did find those things," Marty said, wishing he hadn't as soon as the words left his lips. Marty saw Jack's neck turning red. "Yeah, he found them," Jack said quietly.

At the end of the road, they stopped at a high fence that read:

Stay out. Private Property.

They stared at it not knowing what to do next when someone knocked on Marty's window. They both jumped and Marty let out a yelp. A man looking like Raul, but not Raul, looked them over from the window. He put a finger to his ear and Jack saw the wire coming from it.

"Wait here," he said through the window, his accent almost too thick to understand. When the man left, the wind blew and lifted his sports coat revealing the pistol hidden beneath.

"You sure about this?" Marty asked.

"Ain't much on TV tonight anyway," Jack shrugged. Marty looked over at him. "Yeah, that's real funny," he said, trying to sound braver than he felt. "Seriously," but before he could finish, the man outside had opened the gate wide, waving them forward. "Here we go," Jack said, bouncing his eyebrows cheerfully.

The dirt road seemed to go on forever. They started to worry that they may have missed a turnoff when they saw a clearing ahead. Before they broke through the trees, they could hear the jet engine. When they saw the plane, they stopped the little pickup and stared at it. It was waiting on what looked to be a piece of some abandoned highway.

"I assumed we would meet them at this place and then we would go to the airport," Marty said worriedly. "Who the hell are these people?" he asked, looking over to Jack who was putting the truck back into drive.

"They're people with money, Mart."

"Yeah, but why the plane out here in the middle of nowhere?"

"Just shy, I guess," Jack had to yell it over the loud sound of the jet engines.

Raul came out of the plane and waved them forward, and Jack drove up and opened the door. He hadn't expected the engine roar to get louder and felt like his eardrums would burst. Two men appeared out of what seemed to be nowhere and pulled their bags from the truck. Jack and Marty headed towards Raul, who waved them up the plane's stairs. Marty looked over to Jack and felt the skeptical glance and, truthfully, he was worried as well. He was expecting a long plane ride in coach sitting next to an unwashed Middle Eastern with no sense of personal boundaries. Not a private jet with armed security.

The inside of the plane was richly decorated in Middle Eastern carpets and antiquities. Raul followed them in and closed the door, pulling the ropes that were attached to the plane. The noise level immediately became bearable.

"I trust you had no problems finding us?" Raul asked politely as Jack and Marty looked around at the exotic interior. Jack saw a section to the back that looked like a bar and wondered if they had any cold beer.

"Hey, what's going to happen to my car?" Marty asked Raul. Raul looked Marty up and down over his big, hooked nose before speaking. Marty looked away, finding it difficult to meet the man's eyes.

"You will find that your things will be well taken care of..." Raul paused for Marty to give his name.

"It's Marty Rogers," Jack finally added, knowing Marty had not picked up on the pause. "He's my roommate ... and a friend of mine." Jack looked around and saw what looked to be a reclining chair underneath a fancy red blanket with tacky gold tassels. He plopped into the chair, dropping his backpack next to him. "This is pretty nice, Raul," he said nodding, leaning back, and letting the footrest come up.

"I am so glad you find the accommodations acceptable," Raul answered before giving Marty another look and heading to the pilot's cockpit. Marty turned and found another seat like Jack's and fell into it.

"That guy hates us," Marty said, leaning back and closing his eyes. "You can see it in his eyes."

"I can't see past that huge bulbous nose," Jack said, re-adjusting the blanket underneath him.

"Whose plane do you think this is?" Marty asked, looking around. "This is like from some movie or something."

"I have no idea who owns it, but I'd guess it's probably someone who was getting rich off of my dad's digs."

"So, they hire you in the hope that the proverbial apple, in fact, does stay in the proximity of the tree?"

"Yeah, something like that," Jack answered, looking over at the bar again.

"But little do they know what I know about you," Marty said laughing.

"Oh, fuck you ... pot head!"

"What?" Marty asked in mock innocence before going on. "How are you going to find this scroll thing? Do you even know where your dad was digging?"

"Nope." Jack put his hands behind his head.

"Do you have even a clue how we're going to do this?" Marty sat up, looking around. Just then the plane's engines revved, and they started heading down the makeshift runway. The 'Fasten Seatbelt sign flashed above them.

"Well, there ain't no turning back now," Jack said, looking out the window as the plane left the ground and the images below got smaller as they ascended. He had an anxious feeling but was also excited, wondering what would be waiting for them when they landed. He thought this was probably how his father must have felt every time he left his mother and him alone. The excitement was a bittersweet feeling. He put a pensive look on his face and crossed his arms tightly across his chest in an attempt to hide the excitement, as if it would try to bubble up to the surface and someone might recognize it for what it was.

"The small one is smart," Raul said to the man in the small cockpit flying the plane. "He could prove to be a problem."

"Let there be no accidents, my friend," the captain said, flying with one hand and extinguishing a smoldering cigarette with the other. The ashtray rested on the empty seat next to him. He reached up and scratched at his rough beard. He was thinking that he had spent too much time in the U.S. and it was good to feel hair on his face again. "I do not want questions or any interruptions from our guests," the man said sharply, giving Raul a look.

"I shall see that they are well rested, my…"

"Do not say it!" The captain said between clenched teeth. Raul bowed low, tucking in his arms submissively. "We are not yet home, *Raul*" He stressed the name to make his point.

29

"Yes, of course. My most humble apologies," Raul answered, stepping backwards away from the open door.

"Tend to the good doctor's pup," the man said dismissively, waving a hand and giving the clouds outside his full attention. Raul left without another word.

The smoke billowed out from under the lavatory door. If it had not been for the smell, Raul would have been worried. He had been around Americans enough to know the smell of marijuana and he wrinkled his huge nose in disgust. He ducked under the red curtain dividing the seating quarters from the rest of the plane to find Jack studying a large book. Before the boy realized Raul was there, he read the title. It read *The Great Digs of Egypt, Vol. 6.* This worried Raul more than the smoke in the bathroom.

"May I provide you with refreshment, my boy?" Raul offered smiling. Jack looked up from his book suspiciously.

"We have many assorted alcoholic beverages on board," Raul offered.

"Why are you acting suddenly like Julie from The Love Boat?" There was a burst of laughter and coughing from the bathroom.

"I do not understand that reference," Raul said, taking on a defensive demeanor.

"I saw the bar back there, *Raul*," Jack said stressing the man's name much like the captain had done moments ago without him knowing. "If I want anything I will…"

"It would be an insult to me if I were not to show our guests the proper civility," Raul's face turned red, and Jack saw how important this was to him.

"Okay, fine. I was just kidding around. I will have a beer."

"Ah! Of course," Raul answered, suddenly enthusiastic, and headed for the small bar. "We have many varieties from countries all over the world. We have a Belgian Ale that…"

"Do you have a Bud?" Jack interrupted him. Raul stared at him, still bent reaching for the handle of the refrigerator. "If you don't have…."

"We don't have *Bud*," Raul said, mumbling something in his native tongue under his breath.

Marty came walking out of the bathroom, smiling from ear to ear. "What are you guys do'n?"

"You brought it on the plane!" Jack yelled, looking at Marty wide-eyed. "Do you know what they will do to us if customs finds that shit? You have got to be shit'n me, man." He put his head in his hands. The silence was broken by the sound of a can opening followed by the sound of a beer being poured into a glass. "You boys need not worry,"

31

Raul said, walking over and handing each a glass. "We will not have a problem with customs."

"Don't tell me you have Egyptian customs on your payroll?" Jack asked, now legitimately getting worried.

"No, of course not," Raul smiled. "We will not be going through customs. Please, let us toast to the success of liberating the Scroll of Anubis."

"Interesting choice of words," Jack said, putting the glass to his lips. The beer was bitter, and he had to force it down. Raul looked to Marty and, when he too took a sip, Jack noticed a strange expression come over the face of the Middle Eastern man with the Hispanic name. The man really likes to pour drinks. Raul looked relieved, he thought to himself. He suddenly felt dizzy, and his fingers tingled. He leaned sideways to the arm of the chair, but his elbow fell short, and it seemed the arm of the chair punched him in the face. He felt his eyes closing but before they did, he saw Marty across from him lying on the ground. They locked eyes and as he saw fear, a wave of guilt hit him like a ton of bricks. Then there was only darkness.

CHAPTER 4
FUTURE SITE

Yellow utility trucks sat together lined up, lifeless in the quiet pre-dawn desert. A time long ago, Egyptians believed the sun-god, Re, to be the supreme ruler. As the sun hit the sand, there was no questioning the power. There was nothing around the trucks, sand-colored tents, canvases, or the rolling hills that seemed alive. The site was abandoned. All was silent ... dead silent.

The rolling hills all around could have been the burial place of any number of nobles or even kings of long ago. Unimaginable wealth lay hidden in that sand. But the dusty mummies and ancient artifacts were not the only thing hidden around the trucks and tents. As the wind blew, it uncovered recent corpses decaying without ceremony and riches. It revealed faces locked in silent screams looking up at the sun god as if what the dead men saw there horrified them even in death.

All around were signs of the recent dead breaking up to the surface of their shallow graves. Hands, sandaled feet and faces, dried skin drawn right to the bone lay lifeless and forever frozen in their last moments. The yellow trucks sat just as still. The only difference was that the vehicles were in pristine condition and ready to come to life at the first turn of a key. They were even washed and tuned, waiting at the ready for life to return to them. It was as if the hulking equipment looked on the corpses with disdain for their mortal weaknesses. The sand blew in another direction and almost all of the reaching appendages of the dead disappeared once again as if swallowed by the hungry desert sand.

CHAPTER 5

WENDY

The rumbling of the plane was the only reminder that he was still alive. Jack's body felt like a distant memory and his thoughts were jumbled and incomprehensible as he struggled for consciousness. At one time, he thought the rumbling had stopped but he could not be sure it was not just the darkness he was fighting to take him again. He thought he felt something cool in his hand and, with a force of will, he opened one eye and let the light in. It pierced his brain and immediately the memory of being back in his apartment came to him. He thought of Michelle, Marty's girlfriend in her towel, and the sanctimonious grin on her face. Still, he thought, she did look damn good in that towel. The familiar repulsiveness came to him at the thought. Marty was such a damn fool to be so smitten by her obviously skanky manipulative motives. Marty was such a damn f ... *Marty!*

The thought of his best friend's eyes looking back at him with such terror gave him the strength to try to open his eyes again. The pain was still there but he decided it was better than the guilt he was feeling. He would have taken a thousand hangovers than see that look on his best friend's face again.

"So you live after all," he heard a woman's voice say from beside him. "How divine." Her tone was light but thick with sarcasm. Jack tried to ask who she was but croaked instead and felt the dry pain of his throat. He was so thirsty it hurt. He saw that he was still in the reclining chair.

"I don't understand why idiots like you drink yourselves to death," the woman said, putting a glass of water to his mouth. "To think in college I envied your kind. Drinking, screwing, and having fun all the time." The water felt blissful in his throat. "I can only suspect that most are now regretting their stupid irrational and immature choices."

"The hell we are," Jack wheezed between chapped lips, returning her sarcastic tone. When he looked into her eyes, he knew he had seen her before. It wasn't hard to figure out where. His father had a plethora of young attractive woman *working* as his interns. No doubt, this woman was in one of the group photos Dr. Edwards liked to leave around the house as if to say, 'yup that's right, I'm doing this hot young piece of ass.' As he looked at her there was no doubt her tanned skin was from some tropical beach or tanning salon, not the harsh sun of an Egyptian dig site. He wouldn't even doubt if the long blond hair tied tight behind her was even her hair color. He was sure in this case that the carpet most assuredly would not match the drapes. And undoubtedly the khaki blouse and shorts she wore were some obscure designer label, he thought, disgusted. He glanced down at her shoes and was surprised to see she was wearing well-worn boots on her small feet.

"So … have you seen enough?" She asked, looking down at him frowning as he looked her over. "Let me re-phrase that."

"No need," Jack said, letting his gaze come to her blue eyes. "I have no doubt the late Dr. Edwards has checked out the goods already." The woman's eyes flared, but her face stayed emotionless. He looked over and saw Marty still sleeping soundly.

"I think I liked you better passed out," the woman said, getting up and grabbing the water back from his hands. "By the way," she said over her shoulder, "I think your diaper leaked." Jack did not realize what she meant at first, then he looked down at his pants. They were soaked in piss.

"Son of a bitch!" he yelled, pulling his pants away from himself and trying to get up.

"-Seems the late Dr. Edwards was not paying enough attention to his baby to get him through potty training," she said, pouting her lips sarcastically at him. Jack looked back at her with murder in his eyes. She smiled, turned back, and walked further into the plane. *Oh, I really fucking don't like her.*

Jack cleaned himself up the best he could in the plane bathroom. He had been on planes many times before, but he'd never seen the kind of luxury as this spacious bathroom. The sink and toilet seemed to be made of solid gold. He looked down and wondered what it would be like to shit in a gold toilet. He made a promise to himself to find out. He went to the sink to finish washing his hands and caught sight of himself in the mirror. His eyes were swollen and there was far too much scruff on his face. "How long have I been out?" he asked his image. He couldn't really remember what had happened, but he was sure he hadn't drunk that much. He wanted to check on Marty and make sure he was all right.

Raul watched the whole time through the two-way mirror. He stared into Jack's swollen eyes while taking a long pull from the cigarette dangling from his lips. The long ash fell onto the expensive carpet floor un-noticed. He pulled the safety off his nine-millimeter barretta and pointed the barrel at the boy's head through the mirror. He thought it interesting that it could only be inches away and still the American boy hadn't even a clue it was there. Raul stared into the idiot's eyes, wondering what it would be like to pull the trigger. A smile came to his face as he held the gun, thinking of the boy's brains being blown onto the wall opposite them.

"The time will come soon enough," a voice said behind him. Raul jerked

upright and lowered the gun quickly.

"A thousand apologies," he said bowing his head.

"There is nothing to apologize for," the man said, coming to stand next to Raul and watching as the boy left the bathroom. "The ignorant fools will be judged soon enough." The man scratched at his nearly full beard. "Ala's will shall guide the saber to the western throat ... very soon now, my friend."

CHAPTER 6

THE LAB

The dust swirled around the white jeep as it sped down the rough desert road towards a tunnel that had been cut into the rocky terrain. The road and the tunnel were often used, and the man driving peered through the thin cloth Shimagh that was covering his head and face to see if anyone was behind him. As they entered, he turned his headlights off and on twice. He looked up at the top of the tunnel and counted each light he passed. As he was getting to fifteen, he slowed and started pulling closer to the side of the wall. Just as the jeep seemed about to run into the wall, a piece of the rock wall slid inward and the jeep slipped inside.

The tunnel beyond led to a cage-enclosed elevator. That was all that was in the big room. The man turned off the engine and hopped out of the jeep, fixing his white robe and making sure his face was fully covered. He reached into the back seat of the jeep and pulled a blanket off a man who was lying there blindfolded.

"I would very much like to remove this cursed cloth from my eyes now," the man said in a deep, commanding voice.

"I am sorry, Amir," the man in the turban said politely. "The secrecy is for your protection."

"Yes-yes, can I remove it now?" The man straightened his white robe nervously again, looking around. "Okay, then," he said hesitantly. "But if asked, please say you had it on until we were in the elevator."

"Elevator?" the man said, pulling off the blindfold and squinting, letting his eyesight return. He was a tall, dark Middle Eastern man. He wore an elaborate military uniform that was now dusty and full of sweat from hiding underneath the blanket in the hot sun.

"This way, my Amir," the driver said, pulling a rifle out from behind the backseat.

"Are we expecting trouble?"

"No, sir." The driver opened the cage door to the elevator and stepped inside, holding the door open.

"I would like some water."

"Water and more will be provided soon, excellency."

"See that it is." The man in the uniform angrily crossed his arms. The elevator motor kicked in and he nearly fell over, shooting the other a nasty look.

They traveled far beneath the ground before the elevator ungracefully came to a jerked stop in a small enclosure. There was just enough room for the two to exit and face the large cement door. A lone telephone hung on the wall. The man in the robe picked it up and whispered softly. Just as he hung the phone back up, a slight buzzing sound started and they looked up at the camera above them. It adjusted itself before coming to rest on them. The man pulled the cloth covering his face down slightly. Just as he did, gears began turning and rumbling as the thick cement door slowly opened.

Inside was a long empty hallway with overhead lights that seemed to go on forever. They were alone in the empty hall as the door slowly moved shut behind them. When it shut, the man in the uniform jumped.

"The door is controlled from another area," the man with the covered face told him, bowing slightly.

"How nice." the other in the uniform answered, smiling . Then a small electric car with a flashing red light entered the hall with two passengers. One had a masked face much like the one who had led them here. The other was wearing an expensive suit and smiled brightly. He was not a tall man but had wide shoulders like a man that was once used to lifting heavy equipment or weapons.

"Oh, my dear Ahmed," he said, not waiting for the little car to stop before jumping out. "It has been far too long!" He shook hands vigorously with the man in uniform.

"Khalid," Ahmed answered back coolly.

"We have much to see, Excellency," Khalid said, picking up on the man's demeanor.

"I would like water and a place to freshen up, Khalid."

"Oh yes, of course," he answered graciously, waving an arm towards the car. "Out," he commanded the man in the driver's seat. The man jumped out as if scorpions had suddenly appeared on the seat.

In the small bathroom, Ahmed splashed cool water on his face. He looked at his reflection and the now-filthy uniform. He made a half-hearted attempt to brush off the dust and sighed miserably. Just then, his grooming was interrupted by a haunted, howling sound that echoed off the walls outside the bathroom. Ahmed looked up, catching his reflection in the mirror and jumped back, looking around fearfully. He looked at the door and saw it swinging slightly open.

"Who's there!?" he commanded. The door was then thrown open and Ahmed jumped back.

"Apologies, my friend," Khalid said smiling meekly.

"What by all that is sacred was that horrible noise?" Ahmed asked, visibly shaken.

"That, my friend, is the reason we have brought you here."

"Then you have brought me here under false pretenses," Ahmed said angrily, straightening his dust-covered tie. "I was told I was to see a biological weapon of the future. If that is not the case, then kindly show me to the door."

"Exulted Amir, my dear, friend," Khalid said, throwing up his hands. "Please be patient. We have not deceived you. Perhaps misled … but never deceived."

"What's the difference?" Ahmed asked back, now angrier as the blood was returning to his face.

"The weapon is most definitely biological but not the kind invented in a test tube."

"Plagues? There are ways to battle plagues and that is…"

"It is not a plague," Khalid interrupted. "I will ask you to keep an open mind and to please come with me."

"I am a busy man, Khalid. I do not have the luxury of patience." He looked down his long nose. Khalid simply smiled and bowed, gesturing towards the little white car outside the bathroom door.

After a short ride down the hall, they arrived at another cement door that slid open as they pulled up. Khalid walked in first, clicking on the lights. The room was small and furnished only with a card table and two chairs. Three of the walls were simple dimpled cement while the fourth was covered by a long red curtain. Khalid looked at the camera over the door inside the room and waved a hand absently at the door. It immediately closed. Ahmed looked around the room uncomfortably, thinking that it very much resembled an interrogation room that he himself had used many times.

"If I could point you in the direction of the curtain, my friend," Khalid said, pulling a string. The curtain slowly opened, revealing a window to a dark enclosure inside. Khalid pulled a two-way radio from his belt. "Bring the lights up slowly but leave them low. There is no use getting *him* upset."

"Him?" Ahmed asked, squinting his eyes, and trying to see into the darkness.

43

"Look there, my friend," Khalid said, pointing to one corner in the slowly illuminating room.

Inside, Ahmed saw what looked to be many mutilated human carcasses laying about in different degrees of decay. Most seemed to have, at one time, worn the robed clothing of a Shiite tribesman. "Death is not new to me," Ahmed stated, looking around irritably.

"Back against the wall…" Khalid said pointing, "near the floor." Ahmed stepped closer to the window. As he did, he saw a large canine head rise slowly, its eyes reflecting green in the dim light in the room. Ahmed felt a cold chill run through him as he locked eyes with it. He pushed down the chill with anger. "You brought me all this way to show me a large dog?" he asked, taking a step back from the beast's stare.

Khalid said something quietly into his radio and did not answer Ahmed's question. A motorized sound started, and bright light began to enter the room on the other side of the glass. Ahmed was instantly able to better see the bodies and realized they appeared to be partially consumed by, most likely, the thing inside. He bent down slightly to peer up at the door opening above inside the enclosure. He heard yelling and then he saw the flutter of a man's red Arabic robe as someone fell through the opening above and onto the hard cement with a thud.

"Do you remember the attempt on your life five months ago?" Khalid asked.

"Of course, I do."

Khalid nodded solemnly. "There is your shooter."

Ahmed tore his gaze from the man who now was beginning to move to the short man in the expensive suit beside him. "You are sure it is him?"

"Yes, of course," Khalid said smiling. "But why don't you ask him yourself?" he said, clasping his hands behind his back.

Ahmed looked back into the enclosure and saw the man getting up off the floor and looking at him with hate in his eyes. The man hobbled to the window to come nearly face to face. The man spat onto the window, but Ahmed did not even notice the rude gesture. Instead, he was watching as what he thought was a dog rise up on two legs over the man's shoulders. Ahmed's head rose as he followed it.

"Wha…" he could only get out as he watched the creature rise, towering over the man inside as it came to its full height. The beast opened its huge maw in a snarl. Its black hairy-patched skin rippled with sinewy muscles on its human-like torso. Ahmed bent down to better see the thing's lower body. He saw it was more animalistic than human. It was hunched to spring forward. Ahmed looked to see the man inside turning slowly to see what was there behind him. Before he could, however, the creature lunged forward, slamming the man against the window with what Ahmed thought was an impossible force. The sound of it filled the small room. Ahmed threw up an arm and moved back as the man inside had his face crushed inwards onto the thick glass. The creature looked straight at him for a moment before reaching a clawed hand into the air and swinging it downwards at the man. The window splattered with blood. Ahmed could see only the man's face, still pressed

45

against the blood-soaked glass, moving up and down as the dark shape behind him fed on his flesh. "This cannot be … it is some trick," he said, watching the scene unfold and holding his arm up still, watching the horrific scene transpire before him with wide eyes.

Khalid had not moved before turning away slowly to face Ahmed. "Ah, but it is true. You could ask him," Khalid jammed a thumb at the window. "If he were not being lunch, that is." Khalid frowned and looked at his watch. "I mean dinner. Where does the time go?" He smiled and Ahmed looked over at him.

Ahmed thought the little man's smile no longer seemed disarming but now dangerous. The dead man against the window was suddenly pulled away. Ahmed looked back to see a large red tongue lick a streak through the blood. A golden eye peered through at them. Ahmed felt he was losing control of his bladder and looked away, swallowing hard. "Can you make it stop?" he asked, thinking he would vomit.

"Not without killing it," Khalid answered in a polite voice. "But, my friend," he smiled. "I can hide it." He reached behind the curtain and drew it closed. The beast on the other side howled in rage and pounded the window. "It will-" *Bang* "-stop in a" - *Bang* – "moment." *Bang,* Khalid said smiling.

The Plane

"That's completely ridiculous!" Wendy said from behind the elaborate bar inside the plane, putting bottled water to her lips.

"I'm pretty damn sure we didn't drink enough to lose days, lady," Jack said angrily, searching the plane for his luggage. He had given up wearing his pee-drenched jeans and now wrapped one of the many Afghan blankets around his waist. Marty sat in a chair close by in much the same situation. He stared at his pants, disgusted.

"Where the fuck are my clothes!" Jacked yelled, slamming an overhead compartment closed. Just then, Raul came in carrying their luggage. He set it down, silently smiling.

"Finally, someone civilized," Wendy said, smiling at Raul.

"I trust you have all met?" Raul asked.

"Oh, yes," Wendy said, wrinkling up her nose with distaste.

"Hey, Raul," Jack said, elongating and rolling the "R" off his tongue. "Mind telling us what happened to the last couple of days or so?" Marty got up silently, picked up his bag and disappeared into the bathroom.

"So?" Jack asked again, trying to keep from yelling.

"Mr. Edwards, we are flying at a very high altitude, and that mixed with heavy drinking, could have a very detrimental effect."

"All due respect but … my ass, Raul." Jack grabbed at the blanket that threatened to fall off his waist. "If that were true, where'd Miss Personality over there come from?" Wendy made a disgusted sound in the back of her throat.

"For your information," she began, "You two were passed out when they picked me up."

"We landed?" Jack asked, looking at Raul and trying to not let his mouth fall open.

"Of course, Mr. Edwards," Raul shrugged innocently. "How else would we have collected Ms-"

"Raul…" Wendy chided, mockingly waving a finger.

"Oh, yes. Wendy … my apologies," Raul corrected himself. Jack watched curiously at the look they shared.

"Ain't you two chummy?" he said, stepping forward, picking up his bags, and walking to the bathroom Marty was in. "This is not over," Jack warned, without looking back. Wendy rolled her eyes.

"Shall we discuss it over a drink?" she called back. Raul put a hand to his mouth to stifle a laugh. Jack turned to them and knocked on the bathroom door. The door opened and Marty pulled him in violently, inadvertently making Jack drop the blanket before he was in the door. "Whoa!" he yelled.

"What the hell, Jack?" Marty complained, pacing back and forth. Jack quickly went through his things, finding clean clothes to put on. "What are we into?"

"Don't know, man. But I promise I'll find out."

"I think we're in over our heads here. What are we going to do!?"

"First, calm down, Mart. Don't get so freaked out."

"Freaked out!" Marty yelled at him. "I shit myself! I haven't shit myself since I was like two or something. What the fuck!"

"I don't know, man. But it's all right," Jack said soothingly as Marty started pacing again.

"Maybe Raul's right. Maybe we're not used to flying this high and we just passed out." Jack knew how it sounded but he didn't have anything else to offer. Marty stopped and gave one of his famous Marty looks. He had a way of looking at people as if they were as dumb as dirt.

"What?" Jacked asked defensively. "You're now an expert on the effects of high altitude on the human body?"

"No, but I know the plane didn't crash. So that means whoever is flying this plane didn't pass out for a few days."

"Well maybe the cabin..." Jack stopped when he saw Marty had the look again on his face. "All right, all right," Jack said, throwing up his hands. "Let's just play it out. If anybody meant to harm us, they could have already. Do you agree?"

49

"Yeah, sure," Marty offered, taking a deep breath. "Unless they're waiting to slaughter the pig at the roast," he said, under his breath.

"Let's play it out," Jack said again in the low voice his father used to use when trying to drive home a point. He tried to catch Marty's eye as he paced.

"Fine. As if we have a choice," Marty said at last, stopping and looking at himself in the mirror.

Jack rolled his eyes at him and left the bathroom.

Wendy Ramirez

Everyone who knows her knows that Wendy Ramirez is a hard worker. She was born to a poor white mother and even poorer Mexican father. Her parents had separated shortly after she was born, and she never met her father. Her mother remarried when she was two and, since then, her mother had two more children, her sister and brother. Wendy always felt loved by her mother, but she also felt like she didn't belong in the new family. She was always the outsider and a constant reminder of her mother's youthful mistake. She was independent and, from an early age, wanted to live her life her way. Her stepfather was a kind enough man, but she always thought that he, like her mother, saw her as an outsider to their family.

Being strong-willed and smart, Wendy graduated from high school a year early and received an academic scholarship to a university. There, she breezed through her classes effortlessly and spent most of the time bored out of her mind. She was never the social type and mostly stayed to herself in the large dorms. Several roommates had transferred out of her room saying things like 'nothing personal' or 'it's not you.' But she knew what it was. Most students in the university were not there for the academics alone and Wendy understood their reasons for moving out. But it hurt her more than she would have liked to admit.

All this was, however, before Dr. Edwards's class in Egyptology. There was a chance that she would have never even met Dr. Edwards. She was originally enrolled in advanced calculus with no interest in anything on the history or archaeological side of university studies. It all started when she stopped by the math department's offices to meet with the professor giving the advanced calculus class.

The memory still made the small blond hairs on her neck stand up. She remembered knocking on the door and hearing someone getting startled behind the door. When the door opened and the chubby professor adjusted his glasses on his flushed face, Wendy got the feeling that something was wrong. The little man kept looking down at her chest and not making eye contact. He asked her to come in and, even though something inside of her screamed not to, she had gone in. As she took a seat in front of his cheap gray metal desk, he sat on it close to her.

"What I can I do for you?" he had said in a low, breathy tone. Wendy did not even attempt to make eye contact with him.

"I need to have my registration slip signed to be in your class." Her professor said nothing. "The class is usually for seniors, but my advisor said if you sign it…"

"I'll sign it," he had said, reaching out to her. She reached up with the piece of paper in her hand and the man grabbed her arm. "How badly do you want to be in this class, pretty girl?" That's when she noticed the man was sitting across from her with an erection in his pants at eye level. The man pulled her towards him. She tried to pull away, but he held on tight.

"Now don't get nervous, sweetheart," he had said pulling her. "Let's just have a little fun. We're both adults here, right?" Wendy had not remembered ever being so scared in her life. His grip was tightening.

Wendy leaned forward and the professor leaned back with an excited moan. She then bit the man's arm hard enough to feel her teeth hit the bone. He let out a scream and she took the opportunity to run for the door.

"You stupid fucking bitch!" He had yelled at her as she ran down the hall with the slip of paper falling forgotten to the floor.

She remembered sitting on a park bench outside of her dorm, never feeling so alone. She wanted to tell someone about what had happened to her, but she had no friends. She thought of going to the school dean, but what if they didn't believe her, and she was here on a scholarship. What if they took it away from her ... what would she do then? She wept, sitting there with the weight of it all on her. She remembered how it smelled like old cigarettes and wet dirt there on the bench as she sobbed.

It was through tear-filled eyes that she saw the colorful flyer on the street lightpost across from her that read:

Do you want to see the world off the beaten path? Tired of the same old college routine? Sign ups are NOW for internships in the Egyptology School of Archaeology with Dr. Jonathan Edwards. Three interns will be picked to accompany Dr. Edwards to a dig ... IN EGYPT! HURRY! These fill up fast, folks!

She wiped her eyes clear of tears and immediately went to the archaeology department. The feeling in that building was immediately different. It was full of life as other students waited around for the professors and advisors to be free. She found Dr. Edwards' door and waited outside for the student inside to finish. She heard talking inside and leaned against the wall, looking at all the pictures of artifacts that were there. She had no idea what they were or what they meant. All she knew was that Egypt was far away from everything, and that she wanted to go there more than anything she had ever wanted to do before.

That was when the door opened and a pimpled-face boy came out smiling and running down the hall, most likely late for another class. Wendy remembered taking a deep breath and turning into the doorway, half expecting another calculus-type professor. But what she saw instead took her breath away.

Dr. Edwards had looked up at her, startled, his reading glasses on the end of his nose. His thick hair was graying, and he had deep wrinkles at his eyes as he smiled up at her. "You move like a hunter!" Dr. Edwards exclaimed cheerfully. She stared into his green eyes and felt her heart somersault in her chest. She got chills remembering that day.

Her life had changed in that moment. She threw herself into Egyptology and anything else to do with Dr. Edwards. At first, he did not want her to be an intern as she was not enrolled in the school of Archaeology at the university, but Wendy was too smart and resourceful to let that happen. In six months, she was not only one of Dr. Edwards' best students in the school of archaeology, but also one of the three selected to accompany him to Egypt.

Dr. Edwards and the world of archaeology filled her heart where there was once nothing but an empty hole. Her mentor took on many student lovers, and some she herself strongly disapproved of, but she

54

never judged him for it. She had to admit that if he approached her she would not have turned him away. In fact, she loved him deeply. But she suspected that was one of the reasons he never did come on to her. That and she knew that he knew, that she was becoming one of the best damn Egyptologists he had ever taught. Because of that, Wendy was able to connect at a level none of the doctor's conquests could ever begin to understand. And that was enough for her.

"We are starting our descent to land," Raul announced politely, walking into the area where they sat quietly.

"Landing?" Marty asked. "Already?"

"Yes," Raul answered simply.

"Where exactly are we?" Jack asked, fastening his seatbelt.

"We will be landing in Cairo."

"Great!" Jack said smiling. "Do you know of any place to get a good cheeseburger in 'ole Cairo?"

Wendy made another disgusted noise in her throat.

"No one's talking to you, Barbie," he said, looking out the window.

"Go fuck yourself, Junior." Wendy buckled her belt across from him.

"Ah, young love," Marty said jokingly. Neither Jack nor Wendy commented.

"When we are on the ground," Raul started again like a patient father, "we will be met by some people that work for my employer. They will take uSs to a car where you will be driven to the site where you will begin your search for the croll of Anubis."

"We're not going through customs?" Wendy asked.

"I will join you," Raul went on, unanswering her question. "At the site a few days from now."

"If we don't go through customs, aren't we here illegally?" Marty asked, looking worriedly at Wendy and then Raul.

"All has been taken care of," Raul said simply turning away. "Hold on there, champ," Jack said. Raul stopped and turned with a look of eternal patience on his face. "What is *champ*?" Raul asked.

"It's short for champion. How long is the ride to the site? Are we going to get anything to eat? Who's going to be working for us … besides Miss Sunshine over here, I mean." Wendy gave him an angry look. "I do not work for you," she corrected him. "I was told I was leading this dig."

"Wrong," Jack corrected her. "*I* was told I would be running this party."

"You?" Wendy laughed. "You couldn't run your nose without your mommy wiping it."

Jack scrunched up his face at her like he had just bitten into a lemon. "Listen. I'm not sure why 'ole Raul chose to take you along but I'm sure it wasn't because of your leadership skills … or personality, princess."

"You ever run a dig? Or anything for that matter?" she asked.

"Nope. This will be my first and, hopefully, last time spent on my knees in the hot sun sticking my hands into dirt." Wendy shook her head, disgusted with him.

"Rau-" She started, but saw that he was no longer with them. She looked around but he was nowhere in sight. Marty noisily unwrapped some tinfoil revealing a large brownie.

"Is that … a pot thing?" She asked him, wide-eyed. He took a big bite and looked at her, raising his brow twice.

"I'm a habitual baker," he said, smiling.

"Great," Wendy said, shaking her head. "A spoiled brat and a pothead. You two are going to be just wonderful to work with."

"*For,*" Jack corrected her. "Not *with.*"

Wendy closed her eyes and started counting to ten in her head.

CHAPTER 7

ARRIVAL

When the plane landed, it taxied to a large hanger towards the end of the long runway. The plane pulled into the hanger and Jack, Wendy, and Marty watched from the windows as a man with dark sunglasses and a machine-gun on his back directed the plane inside. Once inside, the engines stopped and they heard the plane door being opened from the outside.

A man in light brown camouflage stepped in and looked at them. He did not speak as he turned quickly and left for the cockpit. They exchanged worried glances back and forth but did not say a word. They heard some talking in an Arabic language in the cockpit and then only silence. There was a sharp hiss of a hand radio and the man said one word that sounded like a grunt. Almost instantly, a man in a flowing white robe and blue turban stepped inside the plane, smiling.

"Ah, Mister Edwards," he said, heading for Jack and taking his hand. "It is a pleasure to see you," he said, shaking Jack's hand vigorously. "I am Siam. A good friend of your father's." Siam put his hands on his hips and looked him over. "You look like a mirror image of the man. Remarkable!" He shook his head in amazement, smiling. "So tell me who your friends here are?" Siam asked, looking around.

"We have met," Wendy said dryly, putting a dusty pack over her shoulder and extending a hand.

"Ahh. One of Dr. Edwards' interns then?" he asked, looking over at Jack and winking.

"Yes, I was once an intern of Dr. Edwards," Wendy said, red-faced and visibly trying to keep her anger in check.

"And who is this good-looking boy?" Siam asked, coming to stand in front of Marty.

"This is my friend Marty who will be assisting me," Jack answered.

Siam looked at Marty, smiling, and shook his hand. "You are most welcome." Marty smiled back and nervously bowed a few times. Siam laughed heartily and merrily patted the boy on the back.

It was another scene outside the plane. Two black, sleek Hummer Limousines waited for them with several camouflaged soldiers with machine guns nervously looking around the hanger. The group of travelers were rushed out of the plane by the good-natured Siam into one of the limos that quickly sped away. Jack looked behind him and saw the other limo take off just as quickly in the opposite direction. He assumed that one held the pilot and the mysterious Raul.

The interior of the Hummer had all the luxuries. The seats seemed to be made of the finest leather and the inside had everything from televisions, faxes, computers, to a chilled bottle of Champagne in a container attached to the side of one of the doors. Siam watched them, silently smiling, as they took in the grandiosity of it.

"So far, this is the best-financed dig I've ever been on," Wendy said, playing with the controls on the armrest next to her. The TV flashed on and off as the mustached, Middle Eastern version of Dan Rather read the news on the screen.

"Our financier is very generous," Siam said, smiling cheerfully into his own thick mustache.

"You mean it's not always like this?" Jack asked, opening the refrigerator and pulling out a Coke. It popped loudly in the confined space when he opened it.

"Oh, yes," Wendy answered sarcastically. "It's always like this. Exactly like this ... always."

"I think I'm changing majors, then," Marty said, laughing. He turned to Siam and asked him if he minded if he smoked.

"I'm fine with it if the others don't mind, my boy," he answered, still smiling. Jack looked to Wendy, and she shrugged silently. Marty reached into the front of his pants, digging around a moment before coming up with a small bag. Inside were several rolled cigarettes. Siam watched him suspiciously as Marty lit the end and inhaled sharply. He handed it to Jack who waved him off. He then offered it to Siam who shook his head with his smile just slightly faded. When he offered it to Wendy, she just stared at him coldly.

"What?" he blew smoke out the now slightly-opened window.

"What if they found that in customs?" she asked, scowling.

"We planned on planting it on you," Jack answered for him smiling across from her.

"Somehow that wouldn't surprise me," she said, her face turning a dangerous red shade again.

"They do this a lot," Marty said to Siam, sucking the smoke deep into his lungs.

They drove for a long time into the brightly lit desert. The city was interesting, and Jack and Marty peered out the windows trying to get a view of the pyramids. Mostly what they saw were busy streets and merchants desperate to sell their wares to the obvious tourists. As they drove to the outskirts of the city, the number of people became fewer, and the buildings looked more rundown. The only colors around the drab buildings were the clothes that hung from lines outside the windows. The car bounced several times into deep holes in the road and they were not oblivious to the cautious stares from the people in the streets. It was obvious that they were not accustomed to seeing expensive automobiles like this, but they recognized the fear on their faces when they thought they had stared too long and looked away quickly, as if something very interesting was suddenly in front of them. As they broke from the buildings and the people, the sands of the deserts went on forever. They drove on and on and several times they had to stop and one of them would run over a hill with toilet paper in their hands. They all tried to get information from Siam about where they were going, but he just smiled and waved them off. Jack thought the strange man was acting more as if they were kids on their way to Disney World rather than going to a hole to look for an ancient artifact.

They sped across the now-darkening desert roads at breakneck speed and more than once they had to grab onto something so as not to bounce off the seat. At one of these points, Wendy was pressed into Jack. Siam watched their apparent discomfort with amusement. This made Wendy angrier, but there was nothing she could do as the car raced across the bumpy dirt roads.

When asked when they would be stopping, Siam just smiled. This got very old as the hours slipped by and the sun went down.

Jack finally lost his patience as he adjusted his seat uncomfortably. "Dude, when-the-hell are we stopping?" he demanded in frustration. Siam looked at him, apparently hurt from his tone.

"My dear boy" he said sadly. "I beg of you to have just a little more patience." Marty snorted in his sleep as the car bounced over something. Wendy had given up trying to avoid touching Jack with the jostling about and closed her eyes but was far from being asleep.

"I need a bed," Jack said running his hands over his face and through his thick mop-like hair. Siam called something up front in Arabic and Jack noticed the driver answered like a soldier addressing an officer. He thought that peculiar and looked at Siam, who smiled his disarming smile again. "We are not far now, my friend," he said, reaching into a pocket in his white flowing robe and pulling out a book. Jack recognized it immediately as his father's.

"Your father mentions the scroll loosely in this paragraph," Siam said, pointing to a section that was roughly highlighted in yellow. "Shall I read it to you?" he asked. But before he could, Wendy started reciting the section. She still had her head back and her eyes closed as her head moved up and down from the rhythm of the jarring road.

"The Egyptians had many superstitions and an endless series of gods and goddesses. Each one of these, had its own relationship to each other, with always a hint of the same context of the high level stories to connect and string the complex plots along. One such story, or legend, is the existence of the scroll of Anubis." Wendy sat up and opened her bright blue eyes. "It is said that this scroll is a hand-written description of the mummification processes by Anubis himself at the time when he and Isis brought Osirus back to the land of the living from the underworld duat, albeit briefly, for the impregnation of Isis, his wife, and which led inevitably to the conception of Horus. This much-disputed text is believed by some to have been written in Anubis's own blood and on the very same bandages that Osirus was wrapped in during his mummification."

Siam smiled, eyes wide. "My goodness!" he exclaimed, delighted. "That was word for word!"

"As I said before," Wendy looked to Jack and then back to Siam, "I was Dr. Edwards' intern for many years." Jack looked at her and saw the prideful look in her eyes. He had to admit even he could not have memorized the words verbatim from his father's book. Perhaps there was more to the pretty intern than met his eye after all. But he had to also admit even a dumb parrot could learn to memorize words that meant nothing to it.

They arrived at a site in the middle of the night. Siam told them that this was not their final destination, but merely a place to rest as they moved on. They were very tired and happy just to be able to stretch. The site itself had little lighting and was covered by a sand-colored tarp held in place by long poles high above them. The camouflage tarp looked to be used to hide the area from anyone looking from above. Large tents were set up in a circle, but they could not see what was in the middle of them.

Siam led them waving encouragingly and smiling as they stepped out of the SUV. Two men appeared out of the darkness and took their bags out of their hands. As they stepped away from the car, it started up again and sped away into the night. Jack and the others turned and apprehensively watched it bounce away on the dirt road.

"Come, come!" Siam waved at them. "Do not be nervous kittens. The cars will return in the morning." Wendy was the first to start walking with Siam. She gave Jack a strange glance that he could not interpret as she passed him.

"I guess we don't have a choice," Marty shrugged, following Wendy.

Jack followed silently, trying to see what lay in the center of the tents. Siam led them to an opening and when they looked, they couldn't believe what they saw. Many tables and servants waited for them. The servants, ten or more, stopped what they were doing and bowed respectfully. On the table was more food than they could have ever hoped for, along with elaborate bottles of any number of things. The tables themselves were low to the ground with elaborate tablecloths and soft pillows surrounding them.

"I'm feeling better about this," Marty said looking around.

"This is most ... out of the ordinary," Wendy said, eyes wide, taking it all in.

"It is what it is, my friends," Siam said, smiling from ear to ear. "Each of you has their own tent ... unless any of you wishes to share," Siam said looking to Jack and winking. Jack looked over at Wendy and met her cold blue stare. "I think alone would be best.," he smiled at her. "For tonight at least." He winked, but Wendy just looked away without comment.

"Certainly ... I will show you to your tents so you can freshen up before you eat." Siam bowed and waved them to follow.

That evening, Jack lay on the soft pillows in his tent that made up his bed. The evening was cool, and he pulled the blankets tight around him. He knew very well what these digs usually entailed through pictures and conversations with his father. Wendy was right that something was going on here. Nobody spends this kind of money on a dig to locate a scroll. Perhaps if it were to find a king's tomb loaded in gold, but even then, there would be little upfront money. He knew there was something else going on and he wished he had not dragged Marty into it. He knew this most likely had to do with his father and his *associates* that he dealt with in moving the artifacts he sold. But if someone was still upset with his father, then why the elaborate campsites and the rest? If someone wanted to get back at Dr. Edwards, then why pamper them?

None of it made sense and he was feeling very tired. He closed his eyes and felt sleep taking over when the silence outside was broken by the strangest noise he had ever heard. It was like a wolf's howl ending in a man's enraged scream. It made the hair on the back of his neck stand up. He was not sure if he had dreamt it. His tent flap suddenly flew open, and he jumped to the back of the tent, gripping a pillow to throw at whatever came through the opening.

"Don't shoot!" Marty said jumping inside. "Those things are *not* toys."

"Asshole!" Jack yelled at him, putting his weapon down.

"What the fuck was that?" Marty asked making himself comfortable among the many pillows.

"What the hell!" Jack complained as Marty started pulling at his blankets.

"I ain't sleeping alone with whatever that thing is running around." If by answer, the howl came again, but this time it sounded closer. "Okay … what-the-fuck is that thing!" Marty asked, pulling the covers up to his face. "Mart, don't be a fag," Jack said pulling his blankets back. "It's just a dog or something."

"That's like no dog I ever heard," Wendy said, coming into the tent. Marty and Jack both jumped as the flap was thrown open. Wendy laughed, sitting down in front of them.

"I need a damn lock," Jack said sarcastically, but smiling at her. Wendy started to say something else but was cut off by gunfire and men yelling. Silence followed and they strained to listen when the tent suddenly lit up. Wendy and Jack nearly hit the top. Marty nodded apologetically and sucked in the smoke from his now lit joint. There were two more popping gunfire shots close by and then silence.

"Are you all in there?" Siam's familiar voice asked from outside the tent.

"Uh ... yes, we are here," Jack answered, awkwardly looking at his guests.

"Ah, good," they heard Siam say with a sigh, which they hoped was relief. Jack noticed that the humor that had always been there was now missing.

"The danger is avoided, and you can all go back to sleep, my friends."

"What was it, Siam?" Jack asked from inside his tent, hugging a red-fringed pillow tight to his chest.

"Just another stray dog out in the desert looking for scraps. It is nothing to concern yourselves about." Jack knew the man was lying even without seeing him. "The men have everything under control, Mr

Edwards. There is nothing to fear out here but the cold desert air, my friends," he said, with the humor now back. But Jack thought it sounded forced.

"Okay, Siam," Jack answered from the inside of the tent. "See you in the morning."

"Will you all be sleeping ... eh, in there?" he asked after a pause. Jack looked to Marty and knew he was there for the rest of the evening. He looked over at Wendy and saw the briefest flash of fear cross her face in the low light from the lantern. She got up and made for the flap.

"Yes, we will," Jack answered, holding a hand up to her. She glared at him, but Jack knew what he had seen. She looked at the ground and flashed a smile before curling up next to Marty. "I will get your blankets," Jack said getting up.

"I don't ..." Wendy started, but Jack was already at the flap.

"I have to piss anyway," he cut her off as he exited.

Outside, the desert air was cold. Jack could see his breath and he wished he was wearing more than just a t-shirt and pajama pants. There were lanterns hanging about giving off little amounts of light. He went a few paces away from his tent and relieved himself. Far off, he saw a fire lit and watched as it grew. He could make out men walking around it with rifles on their backs. The men seemed to be looking around nervously in the darkness that surrounded them. Jack suddenly realized he was standing exposed; he pulled up his pants and went to get Wendy's blankets. He found her tent, grabbed the blankets, and as he moved

68

quickly back, he passed a man holding a rifle. The man was startled and pointed the gun at Jack, wide-eyed. When he saw who it was, he swore something in Arabic and spat on the ground. Jack said nothing but could see the intense hatred in the man's eyes as he walked by him. Another horrific howl broke the night silence and Jack froz,e looking in the direction it had come from in the darkness. He looked over his shoulder and the man with the rifle exchanged a glance before he ran off in the direction it had come from. Jack watched him disappear into the darkness. He could hear someone excitedly talking over the two-way radio.

When he made it back to the tent, Wendy and Marty were sitting up looking around nervously.

"Did you hear it?" Marty asked.

"Yeah," Jack said, tossing the blankets to Wendy. "Just another dog, Mart. Don't get worked up."

"That ain't no dog I ever heard," Marty answered back, hugging his pillow now.

Jack looked over at Wendy and caught her eye. He somehow knew exactly what she was thinking. She was going to say that she had been all over Egypt and had never seen nor heard of any dog like the one they had just heard. Jack could see the words as if they were written on her face. But, somehow, he also knew she wasn't going to say anything because she knew that it would just upset Marty.

"Okay, let's just try to get some sleep," Jack offered. "So much weird shit going on and I'm exhausted."

Wendy silently nodded her approval and rolled herself into her blankets next to Marty again.

"…never heard no dog like that before," Marty complained again, moving around trying to get comfortable.

"Oh, yeah? You ever hear your girlfriend bitch about *our* apartment being dirty?" Jack asked rolling into the pillows.

"Well at least *I'm* getting laid," Marty retorted.

Jack grunted back, embarassed.

Asshole! He thought he heard the faintest sound of laughter coming from the clump of blankets that Wendy was under. *Marty you are such a dick!*

Twice more, they stopped at sites just like the one before. For all they knew they were driving in circles and were stopping at the same site. Siam had stopped driving with them after the first evening. They had by now a barrage of unanswered questions. Like how long before they get to where they're supposed to be digging? And what were the specifics of the site they were going to be digging at? And the question that was in all their minds the most was, what the hell was with all the dog-things in the darkness every time they stopped for the evening?

They had taken to sleeping during the day in the Hummers instead of the tents at night. The evening was spent listening for the howls that would always be answered by gunshots and yelling. Each night, they would sleep together in the same tent. By the third night, it was not even a question. The men didn't even bother setting up the other tents anymore.

Jack felt the SUV stop and struggled to open his eyes. He looked over and saw Marty and Wendy leaning on each other looking very cozy. A flash of jealousy went through him, and he pushed it down irritably. Just then, the door opened and Siam came in smiling.

"Hello, my friends!" he exclaimed merrily. Marty's head shot up in a snort and Wendy looked around confused, with bloodshot eyes.

"I hope everyone is enjoying the journey?"

Jack laughed bitterly.

"Is there something wrong?" Siam asked, sounding hurt.

"When are we going to be there?" Jack asked, rubbing his face.

"We *are* there," Siam answered back, smiling. Jack looked out the window and Marty and Wendy looked out the other side. "Looks like just sand … like everywhere else I've been looking at for days now," Jack said gloomily.

Wendy looked up at the sky and then at her watch. Siam watched her raising a brow. "If I were to gauge where we are-"

"No need, my lady," Siam said, interrupting her. "I will show you exactly where we are on the map when we set up." He smiled brightly at her. "Would you like to see where we will start our expedition?"

"It looks like some giant kids' sand box or something," Marty said, stretching and looking away from the window. "Or a huge cat litter box."

"You are most observant," Siam said, frowning at him. "Shall we?" He opened the door and motioned for them to exit.

CHAPTER 8
THE EXPEDITION SITE

Several pickup truck loads of Arabs showed up as Jack and the others stared ominously at the section of sand that Siam was pointing at. Jack watched as they started to pull things from the trucks and set up tents and tables all around them. He was impressed with how quickly they worked. Siam went on about the importance of the Anubis scroll and so forth, but all Jack could think about was sleeping. He knew he needed to hear about this, but his mind was so tired from staying awake that it was threatening to shut down completely. He heard Wendy's voice, but ignored it as he watched one of the Arabs shout orders and point at yet another rolling hill of sand. He jumped when he felt someone touch his arm.

"Yeah?" he asked, unconciously rubbing the spot where he was touched.

"Siam here has made it pretty clear that you are leading this dig," Wendy said, frowning. "This was not communicated to me when I signed on ... but the importance of the Anubis scroll outweighs any authority misunderstandings ... I suppose."

"Okay. I don't know what the hell you just said," Jack said, rubbing his eyes.

"She said you're in charge, chief," Marty put in. "So, what do we do now?"

Jack turned back and watched a few men disappear over the sand dune that the leader had been pointing at.

"Chief?" Marty asked again.

"You and Wendy go and take stock of our equipment there," Jack said pointing to the men. "Wendy, when you're done could you please join me and Siam here for a rundown of what has been done so far and perhaps to go over a few more details … and mysteries?"

"You got it, Chief," Wendy said mimicking Marty and saluting. She waved Marty to her.

"And knock off the chief, shit!" Jack yelled after them. He watched them as they went off and got engaged in their own conversation, ignoring him completely. He turned back to Siam and saw that he was watching with an amused look on his face.

"Siam," Jack said, crossing his arms.

"Yes, my friend."

"What is going on here?" He asked, hoping he had a stern enough look on his face to make his point.

"Whatever do you mean, Mr Edwards?"

"Cut the crap. What are we in for? What the hell were those *dog* things? And who is running this show?"

"You are in for an adventure that is directly related to your training," Siam said back, smiling. "Your schooling is Archaeology with a focus on Egyptology, is it not?"

"How do you know my father?"

Siam took a deep breath and sighed. Jack was taken aback by the real look of sadness that crossed his face.

"Your father was a dear friend of mine," Siam answered, turning away and looking over the sand. "I worked with him on nearly every dig he had here in Egypt and others. I was a poor digger in the beginning but, over the years, I became a trusted member of Dr. Edwards' team."

"Yes," Jack said, looking at Siam closely. "I think I do remember you from my father's photos. You were much thinner and your mustache was not as gray … but I remember you." Jack squinted, looking at him. "But my father called you by another name … are you … Elvis?"

Siam paused, looking into Jack's eyes. Jack saw the sadness again on the man's face. "I have not heard that in far too long," Siam said, rubbing the back of his hand across his eyes. "When I met your father, I had a Walkman and one tape. I played that tape over and over until I understood every word in English. Well, with my Walkman on I could not hear how loud I was singing. I would sing Elvis songs all day as I worked." Siam laughed. "Your father and everyone else started calling me Elvis. It was an easy name for everyone to remember and before I knew it other archaeologists were asking for me. 'I want Elvis,' or 'we were told to ask for Elvis'."

"Siam. What is going on here? What have I gotten us into?" Jack asked again, stepping closer. He was surprised to see tears coming to the man's usually joyful eyes. Siam looked around the site and stopped looking off in the distance. Jack turned -- and saw a flash as the sun reflected off something there. When Jack looked back, Siam was the joyful tour guide again. He knew there would be no answers now.

"All will make sense soon, my friend," Siam said, taking Jack's shoulders in his tight grip. Siam then laughed loud and pulled Jack into a tight embrace, patting his back vigorously. In Jack's ear, he whispered, "Look for it in your tent."

"What?" But Siam pushed Jack away, laughing again as if he had just remembered something that was too funny to contain himself.

"Oh, thank you, my friend for bringing back those wonderful memories from my youth. I will fondly think of them for the rest of my days!" Siam laughed. "When the tents are set up, join us in the center for our nightly meal. There I will answer any question you may have." Siam turned, still laughing and headed through the sand to where the men were putting the tents together. Jack watched him shaking his head. He was now sure he had gotten himself and Marty into something bad. How bad was yet to be determined, but there was no doubt ... it was bad. He hoped that whatever was supposed to be in his tent would have some answers. He looked around the site and saw that, conveniently, there were no longer any vehicles around. Even the trucks that had brought the men and supplies had left after unloading. He had a sinking feeling this was deliberate. What was so important about a stupid Anubis scroll ... and if

76

it was so important why hire a Mickey Mouse crew like them? It was as if they wanted it to fail … but then why spend all the money to get them here and all the luxuries if they just intended for it to fail? Jack sighed and sat in the sand. He was suddenly very tired again and he rubbed his eyes. There was already sand on his face.

I hate sand!

It was night when Marty and Wendy came back, and the area was being lit by small battery-powered lanterns. As they did every night, the lanterns were dimmed as if they still did not want anyone to know where they were. The three of them ate dinner through yawns and tired groans. Jack told Marty and Wendy that Siam was coming to answer their questions. They were nearly done and yet there was no sign of Siam. Jack probably would have been getting angry at the looks he was getting from them as the time slipped by if it were not for his eyes shutting as he sat on the soft pillows, munching the bread that tasted like flavored cardboard.

Siam came into the clearing, moving quickly. He was wearing fatigues and had a rifle on his back.

"More dogs?" Marty asked, halfway to his mouth with some bread.

"Yes, my friends," Siam said, smiling apologetically. "It seems the animals are very persistent. My apologies, but I must attend to this." A howling broke him off. It was answered by another on the other side of the camp site. They all swivled their heads together, following the noise.

"How big are these dogs?" Marty asked nervously.

"Big," Siam said and turned to go. He stopped suddenly and turned to Jack, meeting his eyes. Without a word, he pulled a revolver from its holster on his belt and tossed it to him. Then he left quickly.

"Oh shit, man," Marty said looking at the gun. "What the hell are we supposed to do with that?"

Jack stared at the gun in his hands. The closest he had ever been to a gun was the one he used with his Playstation at home. He was surprised at just how heavy a real gun was. "Shoot those dog things, I guess."

"You know how to use it?" Wendy asked.

Jack stared at the gun a moment longer. He'd seen enough movies to know this was a revolver type of gun. He knew they usually held about six bullets. He thought people stopped using these in the seventies or something. He looked up into the waiting faces of Marty and Wendy. "I think we should sleep together again. There is far too much weird shit to be separated." He paused and looked at Wendy seriously. "And I do think it best if you sleep nude," he said, straight-faced. "It makes the most sense."

"Yes, I bet it does ... asshole." Jack was surprised when Wendy smiled instead of the expected angry glare. Marty, however, watched their exchange and rolled his eyes, groaning.

"You two don't stop with that I ain't sleeping between you," he said reaching into his pocket. "I don't want to be stuck in the middle when you two horn dogs get together." A howl rang out again, which was immediately followed by gunfire and yelling, just like the other nights. The difference this time was that the yelling was followed by a horrified scream that was broken off abruptly. They stood up looking around them and listening intently. More gunshots, then silence.

"What the fuck, dude?" Marty asked, his pipe forgotten in his hand.

"I'm sure it was nothing," Jack said, just then remembering he had the gun in his hands. He turned it sideways to look at it.

"Dude!" Marty complained. Jack realized that when he turned the gun over it was pointing at Marty's head. "Oh ... sorry, man."

Marty put up his hands and shook his blond dreads at Jack in disbelief.

They stayed together as they prepared for sleep. All their belongings were in Jack's tent. The tent was plenty big enough for them to sleep, but with all their belongings it was getting tight now.

Marty took his position between them, pulling the blankets under his nose. Wendy dimmed the lantern and took off her button-down shirt.

Underneath she had a tight tank top that showed off her curves. She reached up and let her hair down. Jack realized he had not seen her with her hair down and watched, transfixed, as she pulled her fingers through it and tied it up again. She turned and saw Jack watching her.

"What?" she mouthed without saying a word.

Jack shook his head, smiling and feeling a little embarrassed for staring.

Marty rolled over, putting his head towards Jack. "You jiz on me in your sleep you're dead," he whispered, laughing.

"Shut up," Jack said sliding away from him. He felt something hard under the pillow when he moved. He sat up and picked up the pillow. Under it was a book he recognized as the kind his father would use for a journal. There were words on it, but he couldn't make them out in the dim light.

"What?" Marty asked.

Jack put a finger to his lips for them to be quiet. He pulled the blankets off and got closer to the lantern. The words on the book made a cold chill run through him. It read: The Journal of Dr. John Edwards.

"What is it?" Marty asked, sitting up with the blankets still at his nose.

"It's my journal … that's all. I didn't know where I left it," Jack said, opening the book.

"You have a journal?" Wendy asked, sitting up.

"Oh, did I not mention I am actually *not* an idiot?" Jack glared at her and put a finger to his lips. "That's right. My journal. My dad always told me to keep one if I was going to be on a dig." He waved to them, indicating for silence. When they got closer to the light, he pulled the book out and pointed to the name on the book. Marty shrugged and Wendy covered her mouth with her hand.

What? Jack shrugged at her. She leaned close to his ear. He hadn't realized just how good she smelled. "The date runs to after he went missing," she whispered. The words didn't register right away. As the possible realization came to him, he looked down at the book then and up to her again. "You have to look," she whispered, nodding at it. Jack stared a moment more, afraid of what he would find. At times, he had wondered if his father had not just run off with an intern and forgotten him and his mother altogether. They never did find him, so that could be true. He wasn't sure he wanted to see.

He opened the book and folded the pages back to the last page. The handwriting was almost unintelligible. It was almost as if it was scribbled by a child. But on the bottom of the last page was a date. A date six months after his mother had declared him dead. In big letters above the date was one word, carved so deeply into the page that it ripped many below it. It simply read: Hungry.

"That son of a bitch!" Jack whispered, angrily.

"You don't know-"

"Oh, I fucking know," Jack said turning on her. "I know he was alive when my mother was crying herself to sleep every night. I know dear ol' dad was *hungry* when I was getting on my knees every night praying for him to come home." Jack felt the tears coming to his eyes and angrily brushed them aside. "That fucking son of a bitch is probably still out there somewhere stooping another fucking whore!" he whispered harshly.

"Jack." Wendy tried again in a gentle voice. "Maybe if we read more we can figure-"

"How many times did you fuck him?" he asked her furiously. "I guess you hate the idea that he ran off with some other whore and not you?"

Marty sighed deeply. Wendy looked away to hide her face. Jack got up and went to the tent flap. He tucked the gun into his belt. He stopped a second and looked back. Wendy's shoulders bounced as she wept into her hands. Jack lowered his head and pushed through the flap. He knew he had let his emotions get the best of him. He was suddenly the angry teenager again. He hated himself for losing it. He swore and walked away from the tent.

CHAPTER 9

JOURNAL OF DR. JOHN EDWARDS

"Look, Wendy," Marty said, putting a hand on her back as she got control of herself. "It's just that Jack has never really gotten over his dad and … well, you know." Marty found some tissues in his pocket and gave them to her. "You shouldn't feel bad," he tried. "What happened between you and Dr. Edwards is your business. You don't have-"

"Jesus! Marty," she whispered harshly. "You're as bad as the rest of them," she said, blowing her nose.

"What?" Marty asked back, defensively.

"You just assume I was … with John."

"Hey *John's* history ain't exactly secret or anything. And you're … you know."

"I'm what?" Wendy asked, her head snapping up in anger.

"I mean ... you're … come on, are you going to make me say it?" Marty asked, clearly embarrassed.

"Oh, I think I am." She answered, her blue eyes getting wild. "What am I?"

"All right … all right. You're … you know," Marty rolled his eyes at her. "You're pretty is all."

"Oh," Wendy said at last, clearly not getting the comment she was expecting. "Well, thanks … I think."

"Don't mention it," Marty smiled.

"And if it's any consolation, I think you're a prejudiced, judgmental little prick."

"What!" Marty raised his hands in defense.

"That's right," Wendy said, picking up the journal off the ground. "You assume because I'm pretty, as you say, that I would have to be sleeping with Dr. Edwards, right?" Marty didn't say anything. "Well, what if I'm just a damn good archaeologist? What if I just happen to be one of the best in the field? Do I need to be ugly or fat to hold that title? Is that how it works?"

"I guess not." Marty shrugged. "But in my defense, I ain't seen many good-looking archaeologists other than the ones Dr. Edwards had in his photos. But I don't run in archaeological circles. I have to imagine digging in dirt itself don't attract many cheerleader types … like it did when the doctor was around, if you know what I mean."

"Fair enough. Let's just say I do not fit that mold, then," she said, sniffling and turning up the lantern. "Do not judge me without at least getting a chance to know me."

"Good enough for me," Marty nodded. "Not sure about prince charming though ... but good enough for me." Wendy laughed at that. "Do you think we should?" Marty nodded towards the book lying on the ground by their feet. Wendy smiled and reached for the journal.

She read the sentence on the first page. "Everything is going splendidly. The team and supplies have arrived ahead of schedule." She flipped a few more pages. "If the scroll does exist, I am certain we will find it. Everyone on the team is very enthusiastic and ready to put their mark on the world of archaeology. Even Missy is helping-" Wendy made a disgusted noise in her throat seeing the intern's name. *Now, she was a whore!*

"Did you find something?" Marty asked over her shoulder.

"Uh ... nothing yet," Wendy said, flipping the pages again. The date was about a month later where she stopped to read. *"We have found the entrance of a tomb. The hieroglyphics describing the scroll on the walls of Ramses' tomb hinted to its existence and location. We never thought it would be this easy to find. It could be that this is another wealthy merchant tomb ... but I have a feeling it's exactly what we are looking for. Don't look a gift horse in the mouth? How about if it's too good to be true then ... well you get it."*

Wendy told Marty what she had read and skimmed through again until coming to another passage. She read, *"I've got a real uneasy feeling about this. We explored the entrance to the tomb, and it seems from the writings that the inhabitant wasn't exactly buried with high regard. In fact, if I read the markings correctly, this was the tomb of a priest shown*

85

trying to swallow Egypt. Not sure yet what that means. Why do I feel like a lamb being led to the lion's lair?" She read that part out loud.

"So, he already found it?" Marty asked. "So why are we here?"

"Good question," Wendy replied, flipping through the pages again.

Just then the tent flap was thrown open and Jack dived into the tent. He rolled back and closed the zipper and tied the flap tight. He scooted back, pulled the revolver from his pocket and silently pointed the gun at the opening.

"Wha-" Marty started, but Jack gave him such a wide-eyed look at the sound of his voice that he didn't speak again. They heard something walk around the tent and Jack followed it with his gun, trying to gauge where it was. Wendy caught Jack's eye and she mouthed the question *'dog?'* Jack squinted a look at her before hearing what was outside move again and following it with his gun.

The tent pushed in slightly from the bottom and they heard a sharp intake of breath. Wendy pushed away from it towards the center with Jack. The thing pushing through jerked towards her as she moved. Wendy raised her hand as if to smack it, but Jack grabbed her before she could finish. Wendy angrily looked over at him and watched as Jack's head moved up the tent. A cold chill ran through her, and she turned away and watched the thing push through above them. She knew even if a dog was on its hind legs, it should not be able to reach to that height. She looked over at Marty and saw he looked terrified. The thing took another sharp intake of breath and started pushing downward towards Marty's head. He looked over at them desperately.

Jack put his thumb on the hammer of the gun and pulled back on it slowly. When the hammer clicked into place, the tent indent that was nearly touching Marty's head jerked towards him, reacting to the sound. Marty was facing the ground with eyes closed tight. Jack took aim and pulled the trigger ... nothing happened. He looked at the gun and tried pulling harder on the trigger but still nothing. He looked at Wendy, wide-eyed, and she stared back at him helplessly. Jack shrugged apologetically, lifting the gun to her. The thing outside pulled away and the tent popped back into place. They jumped together at the sound.

They watched, waiting for something to happen. When nothing did, Marty sighed, rubbing his face. Then a ripping sound filled the tent. Jack started turning the gun over and over in his hands, frantically trying to figure out what was wrong with it. He looked up and saw Wendy and Marty looking above and he froze. He slowly followed their eyes and saw a tear in the tent with darkness beyond it. Then a large yellow eye filled the hole and looked at each of them individually.

"Oh shit, man," Marty said in a quivering voice. The eye shot towards him. It narrowed and then was gone. They hadn't even realized that there was yelling outside the tent until many seconds later. Gunfire erupted and something snarled viciously. Someone screamed and then more gunfire. The three of them got close together and waited. Another snarl and then a single loud gunshot and something wet splattered the tent.

Seconds later, they heard something heavy hit the ground. There was an eruption of Arabic yelling all around them.

"Hello, my friends," Siam's voice said, just outside. "Is everyone well?"

"Is it gone?" Marty asked in a shaking voice. He looked up at the tear in the tent and a drop of something wet fell through and landed in his eye. He rubbed at it frantically, swearing.

"Have no fear," Siam said soothingly. "The dog has been destroyed."

"That was no fucking dog, Siam!" Jack said, red-faced and opening the tent. He stepped out with Wendy and Marty right behind him. There was a sudden flash of light not far from him as a blaze went up. It was not that close, but the heat was still so intense that they had to back off. Two men with scarves covering their faces and rifles on their backs, went into the tent and started throwing their stuff out.

"HEY!" Wendy complained as her suitcase flew out. The two men came out carrying the rest and dropped them at their feet. Two other men came and poured something on the tent. Siam lit a match and threw it on the tent and it burst into flames.

"What the…!" Marty said, backing away from it.

"Dogs carry disease, my friend," Siam said smiling. "We can't have our archaeologists getting sick."

Jack looked at him closely and noticed his smile did not lead up into his eyes. Siam waved them farther from the fire. They followed him to the other side of the camp.

"This is bullshit," Jack said, drinking the water Siam handed out.

"Your things will be placed in another tent … no problem," Siam said.

"You know that's not what I meant," Jack shot back. "That was no fucking dog. I didn't get a good look at it, but it was no fucking dog, man. I saw it come at me out of the darkness and it looked like it was on two feet. I know how that sounds, but I know what I fucking saw, man."

"Please Mr. Edwards," Siam said soothingly. "There is no need to get excited. The desert, in the light, can play tricks on the eyes. You said yourself that you didn't get a good look. It was nothing more than a stray dog." Jack shifted uneasily, trying to get hold of himself.

"I am sorry you were frightened my friends, but what else could it have been but a dog? There are some jackals, but mostly dogs trying to find some scraps of food."

"How was it able to reach to the top of the tent?" Marty asked, searching the darkness around them with his eyes.

"Dogs can be very clever when they want something. It was probably stepping on something … or standing on its hind legs or some such thing. I assure you, everything is taken care of. Tomorrow we start digging so I recommend you get some sleep, yes?" he asked. "I do not believe we should be..." he stopped suddenly, staring at Marty's face. "Are you hurt, my boy?" he asked, looking at him intently.

"No, I'm fine," Marty said, brushing his dreadlocks back.

"Is that blood on your face?" Siam asked him.

"Dude, I'm fine. Just show me where I'm sleeping. I don't think I've ever been this tired." Marty yawned and rubbed his eyes. Siam watched him without saying a word. "What?" Marty asked, seeing he was still staring at him.

"Hey, what's wrong with this gun?" Jack asked in a low, defeated voice.

"It is old." Siam shrugged.

"Oh, really?" Jack asked sarcastically. "It's old?" He looked and saw Siam had a newer-looking gun in his holster now. "That one looks just fine," he said, stepping up and taking a look. "Let's say I trade."

"I do not..."

"No?" Jack interrupted him. "I'm the leader of this expedition and I say I get the gun." He held out his hand with the old one in his palm.

Siam stared at him for a few minutes before pulling the gun from his hip. "This is a forty-four magnum, Mr. Edwards," Siam explained. "This puts holes in nearly anything. I suggest you know what you are shooting at."

"The holster and clip too, Siam," Jack said, nodding towards his hip. "Don't want one of those puppy dogs out there sneaking up under my little naive nose again, you know."

Jack made Siam go through how the gun worked from loading it, shooting it, and working the safeties. He left nothing to chance this time. When he was satisfied, Siam led them to another tent where they timidly fell asleep without saying another word.

The morning seemed to come as soon as they closed their eyes for the night. They could already hear the bustle of activity outside the tent before opening their eyes. Wendy wanted to tell Jack about what she had found in the journal, but still was not sure how to approach him. She really had no desire to be accused of being a whore again. She knew he was still grieving for his father, but she had never gotten over the disappearance of Doctor Edwards either. Loss was no excuse to act like a spoiled, snot-nosed brat. She had to work her tail off for everything she had ever gotten and this *boy* was acting as if he was above her. She was already making herself angry before her eyes were even open. She sat up and pulled her hair behind her, tying it tight. She felt someone watching her and turned to see Jack's eyes on her chest.

Like father, like son. She thought, disgusted. She hurriedly reached for her button-down shirt and buttoned it quickly.

"Hey," Jack said, still looking at her.

"What." She said, thinking she said it a little angrier than she meant.

"Listen." He started, but then stopped, taking a deep breath. "We're into something here and I don't want…"

"A whore making things worse?" she asked, turning her flaming blue eyes on him.

"I didn't say that."

"Didn't you? Because I seem to remember that that was pretty much exactly what you said."

"I know … and I'm sorry," he said, sitting up.

"Why?" She asked, crossing her arms.

"What?" He asked back, confused.

"Why are you sorry? Because *we're into something here* as you say, and we don't need the whore causing more trouble?"

"Hey. I'm just trying to say-"

"Yeah, whatever Edwards. I think you've said enough." She got up and pulled at the tent zipper. "You know what," she went on as she worked the zipper. "You, like the rest of the world, are always ready to judge me as soon as your eyes are on me." She pulled the zipper up and the tent filled with bright light. Wendy paused, taking in a deep breath. "I think you need to save the tantrums for awhile and see what's in that book." She started to step out, but then paused again. "And whatever you're small, perverted mind may think of me, Jack," she sighed, "I lost somebody too." With that she left, pulling the zipper closed behind her.

92

Jack fell back onto the pillows with his hands on his head. "Thanks a lot, dad. You get the goods and I get the baggage."

"Dude, give her a break," Marty said, deep within the blankets. "She's really not that bad if you give her a chance."

"Work'n for the enemy now, Brutus?"

"Oh, kiss my ass." Marty sat up, scratching. "You know what the problem with you two is?"

"This ought to be good," Jack groaned.

"You two are so much alike it's weird. Just tell her you like her already and maybe she'd be less apt to kill you in your sleep."

"Like her!" Jack yelled at him, wide-eyed. "Are you kidding me?"

"Nope." Marty smiled. "I've known you forever, dude. And I know what I know, and you've got the hots for the *goods* yourself."

"Say that again and I'll call the puppies," Jack warned.

"That ain't funny, man," Marty said, unconsciously picking up a pillow and looking at the top of the tent where they had seen the big yellow eye.

CHAPTER 10
TOMB OF ANUBIS

Siam showed them the many scripts, scrolls, and maps on the table near where they thought to begin digging. It was a simple card table with a blanket covering it. They faced a hill that had a ridge on the other side. Jack had no idea what he was looking at, but Wendy started flipping through, frowning. Jack felt a pang of jealousy as she obviously knew what she was doing as she went through the motions. He knew she didn't care about the things she was staring at. They had talked late in the evening yesterday, and she had shown him the journal and he read it knowing he had made a big mistake. The tomb had already been found. And from his father's journal, it was found even before he got there. Something was happening here, and they were somehow a part of it.

As he listened silently to Wendy and Siam talking about geometric search tools, his mind went back to the passages toward the end of the journal. It sounded as if they had starved his father to death. The entries started to become more infrequent and almost unintelligible. The very last word carved into the pages worried him. What kind of monsters were these people that he had volunteered to work with? What had he gotten himself and Marty into? He looked down at the sand at his feet and could see the word there as if someone was carving it out in front of him. It was simply the word: *Hungry*; barely legible and carved through many pages as if by some sharp knife.

Did they starve him? But even if he was starving, why all the scribbled words and meaningless drivel? Could he have been poisoned? Why would someone want to poison an archaeologist? Though Jack had to admit his father had made enemies with his extra-curricular activities with the Egyptian booty. Why all the expense of bringing his father here and digging up a tomb that was already found? If they wanted his father dead, easier to just shoot him?

He suddenly heard his name and snapped up, looking around. Wendy shook her head, sighing and pointing at the map on the table. Jack couldn't help but be impressed by the way she still acted as if they had never found the journal. He looked into her eyes and saw the fear, but he knew if he weren't looking for it he would have missed it.

"Jack, please," Wendy pleaded, pointing to a spot on the map. "If we are to find this, we will need your attention at the very least."

"Don't get excited, Indiana Jones." Jack stepped closer to the table. "Where was my father digging, Siam?" he asked, wondering if Siam thought his jibe at Wendy sounded forced. He worried that he was not as good an actor as she was.

"Ah! Very good, my boy. Cross out the places we have been first to rule them out." Siam slapped Jack on the shoulder. "Seems there *is* much of your father in you!"

Jack looked over and saw Wendy rolling her eyes. He thought it seemed so natural and that even she wasn't that good of an actor.

"There are marks on the map that describe the places that have already been investigated," Wendy said, straightening her shirt and crossing her arms. Jack looked down and tried to get an understanding of what the map with all the lines and shapes meant. He followed the small, penciled x's as they moved around the map. A slight breeze blew, and Wendy stepped forward to help hold down the map. Jack stared, trying to find a pattern to the marks. As his eyes traced one of the lines, there appeared to be a smudge on the map. He reached out a finger and felt the spot. It felt as if someone had erased a mark there and taken off some of the paper of the map as they did. He looked up at Wendy and she too looked at the spot knowingly. They were even using the same map his father had used to find the spot. Whoever was running this show was sure they were idiots ... or didn't care if they were figuring things out.

"How about here?" Jack asked, knowing it was the spot. His heart skipped a beat as it would right before a rollercoaster started its descent down the tracks. He could almost hear the clack of the wheels on the tracks as Siam stepped forward and looked. He smiled and nodded his head. Tack! Tack! Tack! The rollercoaster started to pick up speed.

"We shall start there immediately," Siam said, walking away and shouting orders. Jack imagined he could hear the screaming as the coaster took off at full speed ... straight down.

Wendy casually looked around to see if they were alone. "Even they can't think we are that dumb ... could they?" she asked in a whisper, pretending to be concentrating on the map.

"I think they do," Jack answered, pretending to be tracing something with his finger. "And if we did not get that journal from Siam, who knows what we would be thinking right now."

Wendy grunted in agreement. "Should we check on Marty?"

"He's fine. He probably just wanted to hang back and enjoy some of his brownies."

Wendy laughed slightly and Jack thought it sounded nice. He looked up into her eyes. She looked over at him, confused. "What?" she asked, looking around.

"I really am sorry, you know."

"Forget it."

"I won't. I'm a jerk."

Wendy looked back down at the map nervously. "Well, there is no point in denying that."

Jack could see the slight smile on her face and felt a little better. "We've got to get out of here."

"I'm not even sure where the hell we are," she whispered back, picking up an instrument and tracing on the map.

"Maybe we could steal one of those digger things?" Jack asked, looking across the site.

"Won't get far in that. It guzzles gas and there are miles and miles of desert out there. We'd be dead in a day in the hot sun without water."

"You got a better plan?" Jack felt anger rising to the surface.

"You're the leader," she answered back, stepping around the table as if she had found something interesting.

Jack paused, getting his anger in check. "We find the site and start digging until we figure something out," he said, grabbing a bottle of water that was sitting nearby. "In the meantime, we do not let on that we know ... that we know. So, continue with your sweet demeanor, sugar."

"Fine."

"Fine."

The trucks rolled into the clearing like a rumbling army. The spot the team had decided on was marked by a small orange flag in the sand. As the big pristine digging equipment began their removal of the sand, Jack couldn't help thinking how different this was from the fantasies he had of his father's digs. There he imagined rows of workers filling baskets of sand. He even imagined in black and white, like some of the old movies he had watched. He had seen some of the photos his father had taken, but for some reason he still had the old celluloid image fixed firmly in his mind. This just seemed to kill the fantasies he had about what this should be. Not even to mention the weird creatures in the night and the feeling that they were lambs being led to the slaughter. This wasn't at all what he thought this was going to be. He wanted the degree but not at the cost of his and Marty's life. Now there was Wendy also to consider in the mysterious equation.

A thankful breeze blew, and Jack closed his eyes and let the wind tickle his perspiring skin. He thought he heard someone speaking over the noise of the trucks, but he couldn't resist taking full advantage of the blissful wind in the hellish heat. He heard the voice again and sighed, opening his eyes and looking. Marty, who seemed to have been dying from some cold or something hours ago was now enthusiastically pointing to a hole in the sand that the trucks had made. Jack shook his head and closed his eyes again, but the breeze had moved on and all that was left was the excruciating heat of the sun. He pulled off his blue faded baseball cap and wiped his forehead with his arm. This only made his head wetter from the perspiration on his arm. He swore and squeegeed the wetness off with his fingers.

I hate this hellhole of a place!

"What is it, Mart?"

"There is something there!" Marty pointed in the hole, smiling like a dog who had found a bone in the dirt.

He and Wendy had decided it was best not to share much more with Marty as not to get him too riled up. They had nearly gotten through the journal in the last couple of days, and what they had found was less than comforting, to say the least. When Marty recovered from what he had probably picked up from some runny-nosed Arab around the camp site, Wendy and he tried to make sense of what was going on.

99

As far as they could glean out of his fathers' journal, the whole expedition was just a cover up for poisoning him. It made no sense, but that was the only conclusion they could come up with. Dr. Edwards caught on that something was wrong early on, but continued on with hopes of finding the scroll, regardless. It was when his father actually entered the tomb of Arakis, which was the name of the priest that was buried there, that things got confusing.

Apparently, his father had entered the tomb as at five and left it at two. The pages that would have explained that are ripped out of the journal. All that was left were slight explanations of the text on the walls and some of the findings in the tomb, which Wendy found fascinating but spoke little of as she stared at the pages with a perplexed look on her face. It was almost as if Siam had left the pages that kept them looking for the scroll and purposely taken out most of what described what happened. All that was left was his father's sentences here and there about becoming more ill as time went on. His failing health was described in a way that made Jack and Wendy both cry. His father had obviously suffered greatly. The almost unintelligible words spoke of a skin-eating poison that obviously took over the mind as well. It left the victim in such terrible pain and dementia that his father thought the only thing that would help was food. He apparently begged to be fed again and again. It got so bad at the end of the journal that his father wrote in a scribbled way about attacking, and if they read the words correctly, even consuming his captors. After that the only word left was the carved word: Hungry.

Wendy had moved closer to the hole in the sand. She turned to catch Jack's eye and waved him over. Jack remembered a passage in the journal where his father said he felt like a mouse being led to the lion's lair. He sighed and walked over to her. When he climbed the mound of sand, nearly falling twice, he stood next to her looking into the darkness of the hole as the big yellow bucket of the backhoe went back in for more sand. Wendy touched his arm and he looked over. There was no use talking as the trucks were making far too much noise. She looked down at her foot then back to the trucks again. Jack looked down and she moved her foot slightly. Underneath was what looked like the top of a backpack. Jack looked away again quickly so as not to draw too much attention to it. As the backhoe came up, Wendy pointed to what looked like a rock ledge starting to be exposed. Jack nodded enthusiastically, not even really seeing what he was nodding at. He wanted to get that backpack. But how? How was he going to pull that pack out of the sand right there in front of everyone without them noticing? Marty came up next to them, smiling and pointing into the sand. Jack smiled back, nodding. He thought then that his friend must look like a damn fool with his dreadlocks bouncing, pointing at a pile of sand. He looked like some crazy muppet bouncing up and down. If someone didn't know him, they would think he was a complete idiot. For some reason, Marty always hid his true identity under dreads and the garb of a burnout so no one could see what was really going on. It was one big cover-up.

One big cover-up. Cover it up! You're the man, Mart!

"Hey dude," Jack yelled into Marty's ear. Marty nodded for him to go on. "Do me a favor and get a blanket and an umbrella for this sun. We'll sit up here a while and watch."

Marty started to object when Jack gave him his deadpan stare. Even with the sound of the trucks, Jack thought he heard his best friend's groans of annoyance.

Minutes later, Marty came back with a blanket, an umbrella and what looked like a makeshift grinder sandwich. As Jack looked over at him, Marty winked and took a big bite. He smiled with all the food stuck to his teeth. Jack shook his head, laughing.

I will get you out of here. I'll get us home, I promise.

Jack grabbed the blanket and umbrella. Wendy looked at this dubiously. Jack winked and pulled her back a bit. He lay the blanket out over where she was standing, sat and opened the umbrella and watched the hole as it got bigger, revealing more of the ledge. He indicated for Wendy to sit. She looked at him, raising a brow. Jack patted the ground and winked. She laughed a little and sat on the other side of the blanket. Jack nudged over towards her with umbrella in hand. She watched him move over with her brow furrowed, not knowing what he was up to … and not sure she trusted his intent. He put the umbrella over both of their heads and watched the digging again. He looked over at Marty, who was in mid-chew and watched them with a surprised look on his face. Jack shrugged a 'what' and turned back to the hole.

Somebody yelled and the digging equipment shut down all at once. They started looking around to see what had happened. Jack saw. Behind them, Siam was walking towards them fast. He nudged Wendy and nodded in his direction; she turned, and they stood.

"My friends!" Siam called out waving. "I believe we have found an entrance to a tomb!" he said dramatically, as he climbed up the mound of sand.

"Really?" Jack mumbled under his breath.

Wendy bumped him with her elbow.

"This could even be what we are looking for!" Siam said, smiling widely. "The tomb of..." Siam stopped then, eyes wide, realizing what he was about to say. There was no way anyone should know what tomb was there in the hole ... unless they'd been there already. Wendy crossed her arms and looked away, trying to hide her anger.

"We should go back to the tents and discuss out next course of action," Siam offered in a more subdued way now.

"Yes," Jack answered. "Lets all get back to the tents and discuss what we do next." He waved them forward and turned back for the blanket.

"Leave it," Siam said waving him over. "I'll have someone pick it up later.

"No, no," Jack reached down and, with a firm grip, grabbed onto the backpack below the blanket and sand. He pulled it up but the backpack did not give. He pulled again, trying not to show his straining. He acted as if his back was aching.

"All this sleeping on the ground," he said lamely as he pulled again with everything he had. The pack seemed to be caught on something but was coming free slowly. Jack stepped forward, letting the weight of his body pull the pack the rest of the way free. He walked down the mound as if nothing had happened. Jack hoped there was nothing that would be dragged behind the pack to give him away. As he walked past, it seemed his ruse had worked.

Siam watched him as he passed and looked over to where the blanket had been. Just visible was a corpse's bony arm sticking out of the sand. Siam walked over and looked at the face half buried there. It was nearly a skeleton with long blond hair blowing in the breeze around it. Siam kicked dirt on it as he looked around. He saw men standing by one of the trucks and waved to them. He pointed once to the sand at his feet and followed the others to the tents, smiling again.

Clever boy.

"Where'd you get that?" Marty asked, pushing some reddish fruit into his mouth.

"It was buried in the sand. Wendy found it by the dig site."

"It has our school logo on it. Why does it have our school logo on it?" Marty asked with full cheeks.

"Let's take a look and find out, shall we?" Jack asked, struggling with the zipper to open it.

"It looks like a designer backpack." Wendy said, getting closer to it. "There's even a place here to plug in an MP3 player. I think I know whose this is," she said ominously.

"I can't get this damn thing open."

"Trouble with your things?" Siam asked, poking his head into the tent. All three of them jumped, nearly hitting the top of the tent.

"Dude! Not cool!" Marty said, choking on the food in his mouth.

"No need to be so jumpy, my friends." Siam smiled. "It is only your friend, Siam!"

"Yes," Jack said, frowning. "How about we talk about our friendship, shall we? And maybe about a little something else while we're at it."

Siam's eyes got big, and he silently waved at them frantically. They exchanged confused glances.

"Why don't we all step outside and say hello to a familiar friend of ours, shall we?"

"A familiar friend?" Jack asked, confused.

"Please, if you would step from the tent," Raul's familiar voice said coming from outside. "I would be much thankful."

"Raul!" Wendy yelled. "Oh, thank God." She jumped through the tent flap, nearly knocking Siam over. "Oh, I can't tell you how glad I am to see you!" she said, giving him a hug. Jack stepped out of the tent and watched as Raul uncomfortably patted her back. He was not sure if the big-nosed man was trying to be reassuring or if he was trying not to be sick from total repulsion.

"We need to speak to you right away," Wendy went on. "I have so much to tell you. Can we speak?" she asked, pulling Raul's sleeve away from them. Raul did not move. Wendy tugged a little harder before looking up, confused. Jack glanced over at Siam and saw him looking at the ground with a strange look on his face.

"What is it, Raul?" Wendy asked, trying to make eye contact. Raul stared straight ahead as if suddenly becoming a statue with a very well-endowed nose.

"I will ask you to not pull at my clothing, Amer-" He stopped again, and Jack realized the man was trying to hold back rage. "Please stand with your friends," he said in that ever-patient voice he had used on the plane.

"Raul, what is wrong?"

"STAND THERE!" he yelled and pointed. It was in such a commanding voice that all of them jumped, including Siam.

Wendy quickly moved over to Jack and Marty, eyes wide and filling with tears.

"Thank you," Raul said, sighing and smiling slightly. "I do not mean to be short, but time is passing, and I do not have much of it." He looked them over one at a time. "None of you look the worse for wear. What have you found out so far?" He looked into Jack's eyes and waited.

Jack swallowed and was unsure exactly how to answer. Did he know about his father's journal? Even worse, was this man the one who was behind doing all those horrible things to his poor father? Perhaps, if he answered wrong, would good 'ole Raul pull out the gun that was making that bulge under his coat and kill them all right here?

"Using the maps Siam had provided…" Jack swallowed and tried to wet his mouth with his now sandpaper-like tongue. "-we have determined what we think is a probable location for us to begin our digging."

"And you have begun?"

"Oh, yes." Siam answered for him. "We have made very good progress."

"What have you found?" Raul asked Jack. Siam started to answer again but Raul raised a finger and Siam fell silent.

"We have uncovered a ledge of stone. We are planning on investigating it after lunch."

Raul frowned deeply. "This is an archaeologist find of the century. Cannot your stomachs wait for just a short while?" he asked. Jack was sure he saw hatred flash across Raul's eyes as he looked at them.

"My team needs to be fully prepared for what may wait for us in that hole," Jack said, returning Raul's stare. "Besides, whatever is down there has been there for thousands of years ... what's a little tuna fish and potato chip sandwich gonna hurt?"

Raul walked up to the tent and reached in. He pulled out the backpack they had pulled out of the sand.

They nervously looked at each other.

"You will go now," Raul said, pushing the pack into Jack's arms.

"Or ... we could just go now," Jack said back, smiling. "No problem."

"Raul," Wendy started, "I do not understand why-"

"It is not important for you to understand, Ms. Ramirez. It is only important that you do as you are told."

"Excuse me?"

Jack saw the now-familiar glare in Wendy's blue eyes. He reached for her, but he was too late. She marched up to Raul's face.

"I do not know who you think you-" Raul's hand flew up almost too fast for them to see it. Wendy was lifted off the ground and landed on the hot sand, holding her jaw.

"HEY!" Jack yelled, stepping forward. Before he went another step, he heard the rifles behind him cocking. He slowly turned to find four men in white robes and covered faces aiming rifles at his back.

"This was not in the brochure, *Raul,*" Jack said, feeling more angry now than scared.

"Jack," Marty said, frightened. "Let's just do what he wants."

"What do you want?" Jack asked Raul.

"Simple, Mr. Edwards. I want you to locate the scroll of Anubis. Perhaps you should start there." He gestured towards the hole in the sand.

Just then a howling filled the air. Everyone stopped and looked in the direction it came from. Wendy got off the ground and stood next to Jack. Then there was another howl from another direction. Then another and their heads moved like some morbid tennis match as more cried out. This was the first time they had heard them in the daylight.

"This is not how it is to happen," Raul said to Siam.

"I cannot control them," Siam said back, glancing over at Jack.

"Get them into the tomb and exterminate the creatures."

"Creatures?" Jack asked. "I thought they were dogs."

"Enough of your banter, boy," Raul said, pulling a cigarette from his pocket. "Get into that tomb now or I will shoot him." He pulled a gun from his hip and pointed it at Marty's head.

"Okay-okay!" Jack yelle,d holding up his hands. "Everyone, grab your things and let's go."

Gunfire erupted around the campsite. Men started yelling and then screaming.

"Get your things and let us go now!" Siam pushed Wendy, who was closest to him, towards the tent. She dove inside, grabbing her pack and jumped out. Marty kept looking around, terrified. Jack started for the tent, but Siam grabbed his shirt and pulled him back.

"Too late. Let's go!" he said, pushing him towards the hole in the sand. Marty moved quickly next to Jack.

They ran for the opening with bullets whizzing in the air everywhere. Siam spoke into his hand radio as he ran. As they got to the hole in the ground, men were already moving sand away from what looked to be a square stone inside the ledge. Before jumping in, Jack looked back and saw Raul firing his gun at something on the ground near his feet. He still had a cigarette in his mouth, and he looked up at Jack, meeting his eye. Jack could not see what was on the ground, but he was sure it was not a stray dog.

"Come on!" Siam said, pulling him down.

Men lay around the top of the hole with rifles, firing frantically. From the corner of his eye, Jack could see one man pulled out of the hole and disappearing beyond. As he watched, another screamed and disappeared. Blood and what looked to be pieces of flesh flew back in and landed right where the man had just been lying.

110

"It's open!" Siam yelled, grabbing Jack and pulling him towards the rocks. Jack tried to look up at the top of the hill again, but was pushed through the dark entrance.

"This bag has some supplies," Siam said, throwing a bag to him. "I will come for you as soon as I can." Siam turned to leave, but paused and turned back. "Do you have the pistol?"

"It's in the tent."

Siam pulled his free arm and stepped up to him. "I had no choice," Siam said sadly to him. "He has my children." Siam stuffed the gun into Jack's pants. The screaming continued outside. "Do not have contact with any part of them and you will be safe."

"Them?" Jack asked.

"No contact," Siam warned, pointing at him with a stubby finger to make his point, then he turned and ran out of the entrance. Immediately, the rock was pushed into place and they were in total darkness. They stood still for several moments, listening to the now-muffled battle raging outside. There was a click, and they could see again.

"I'm starting to seriously rethink my career path," Wendy said, running an arm across her mouth. With the flashlight, she looked at the blood that was now on her arm. "Great," she said, looking at it angrily.

"I'm sorry, Wendy," Jack said, coming to stand next to her.

"Sorry for what?" she asked. "You didn't hit me."

"I know … I'm just sorry, you know?"

Suddenly there was a new flickering light. They turned to see Marty lighting a pipe and taking big inhales.

"What?" he asked, trying not to let out too much breath as he held the smoke in.

CHAPTER 11
RAUL

Raul shifted uncomfortably in the back of the black limousine. He punched the number into his cell phone, trying to ignore the repeated gunfire outside. He sighed deeply before putting the receiver to his ear.

"My Prince."

"Yes, I have arrived. There seems to be a slight ... inconvenience."

"No, I will make sure it is dealt with and things continue as planned."

"I understand. No, I will not disappoint. I will see that the Edwards boy finds the body and is introduced to it properly."

"Yes, Siam is doing his part."

"Both of them, my prince?"

"He will be very saddened to hear that."

"No, I will not let him know until his part is finished. He will not be ... easy to deal with when he hears of this news, my prince."

"Yes, I will do it myself just as soon as it is appropriate."

"Both Americans as well?"

Raul held the phone away from his ear as the person on the other side yelled. Raul gingerly brought it back. "Your will is my command. All shall be done." Raul turned off the phone and put it back into his pocket. Suddenly, the car shook and something walked on the top. There were gunshots and then blood dripped down across the windows on either side. Raul leaned back and pulled out another cigarette. He lit it and pulled his gun free. He released the magazine and set it aside. He reached down and touched a button underneath the seat, and it popped open with more guns and ammunition. He pulled a full magazine free and put into the gun. He made to close it but paused. He reached down and grabbed another and found a long, curved knife that he stuffed into his pocket. He closed the drawer.

Raul reached into a pocket and pulled out black leather gloves. He put them on and opened the door of the car to the chaos. Fires were being started everywhere as the men burned the dead … and sometimes the dying. He heard a flop next to him and he saw the men had pulled the one that had attacked the car off and were setting it aflame. Raul came to stand next to it. Most of its head had been blown away and he could only make out the eye on the lower half of the jaw. The fangs were long and sharp, and the eye stared up at him. He looked over the body and saw that it had breasts.

"Have you burned what is left of the village?" Raul asked one of the men standing ready to spray the gasoline.

"Sir, there is nothing living left."

"That is not what I asked you."

"We did not see the need to burn it as it is abandoned."

Raul fixed the man with a stare, and he took a step back. "Our pardon, we will burn it immediately."

"All of it. Make sure nothing remains untouched by the flame."

The man nodded his acknowledgment.

"You will not live to see my reaction the next time you do not follow my orders," Raul added, before turning away to find Siam.

CHAPTER 12
TOMB OF ARAKIS

"What now?" Marty asked, looking around the dimly lit room. Jack turned on one of the battery-powered lanterns that Siam had left for them.

"This is amazing," Wendy said next to one of the walls, running her flashlight across it. "There were hints that this may have existed but…"

"What do you think those things were?" Marty asked. "Jack?"

Jack sat with his back against the rock that was their door and tried to get the image of the men being pulled over the ridge out of his mind. He knew something horrible was out there … and it wasn't a fucking stray dog!

"Dude … I just don't know … I don't know." He shook his head but it still buzzed with the images.

"This is like some kind of bad dream or something." Marty slid down the wall to sit next to him. "I mean, this stuff just doesn't happen to people … does it?" He looked around but nobody seemed to be noticing him. "No, it can't. I mean what are we talking about here?" Still, no one looked at him. "Are there like American Werewolves in London now vacationing in Egypt? I mean, what the fuck, man!" He looked around and now he had all their attention.

"Mart, that can't be, and you know it," Jack said, putting his head back and closing his eyes. "It's daylight and werewolves only come out during the full moon."

"That's not funny, man!" Marty complained. "It's not ... at all."

"Come on Mart. Smarty Marty ... you know there is no such thing. Use what's left of that big brain of yours and ask me your ridiculous question again. There is not and never have been werewolves. They are made up things to sell movie tickets. Come on dude! I need you here!"

"Actually," Wendy interrupted, "The idea of half man and half animal has existed for as long as at least we were able to draw and paint."

"What?" Jack half opened his eyes.

"You said the idea of werewolves was created to sell movie tickets."

"So."

"So, I'm telling you that that statement is not entirely correct. That's all." Wendy continued to trace the walls with her flashlight.

"So, you think maybe we can skip the history lesson and get to something maybe more useful like ... hell, I don't know ... maybe like WHAT THE HELL DO WE DO NOW!" Jack yelled.

Wendy turned around and gave him a disapproving look. "The things in the tomb are thousands of years old. Please show some respect. Who knows what kind of damage your shouting could do."

Jack's mouth fell open, looking at her in disbelief.

"What?" she asked.

"After all we've been through, you still give a damn about some long-dead old guy and his stuff?"

"His *stuff* are clues into the past and are most likely worth more than any of us can imagine."

"Worth more than our lives? Are they worth more than that? Is that what you're thinking? 'Cause if you are, then I'm thinking you've been tying that ponytail too tight for too long, sweetcakes."

"Fuck you."

"Fuck you!" Jack shot back, getting up. "And while we're at it, how about you tell me why you and Raul seemed so chummy before he laid you out, huh? What's that all about? Care to elaborate?"

"I don't answer to you, little boy. Don't you even think that I owe you *anything*?" Wendy retorted, her blue eyes shimmering bright with rage in the dim light.

Marty watched them stare at each other, inches away, without saying a word. He didn't know whether they were going to punch each other or start making out. He saw the backpack that Jack had pulled from the sand and pulled it closer. He tried the zipper and shrugged, remembering the hard time Jack was having, when it opened easily.

"He made me believe…" Wendy stopped, looking away for a moment. "He made me believe I was a friend." She swallowed, gaining more momentum. "He told me he would help me get established in the archaeological field so that I would one day have my own digs." She swallowed a lump in her throat before going on. "So that I wouldn't just be the pretty face that no one takes seriously. So I wouldn't just be 'one of Dr. Edwards interns.'" She made her version of a man's knowing laugh before going on. "You can't possibly know what it is like."

"You can't possibly know what it's like living in the shadow of the legend," Jack added leaning back.

"Seems we both are living under that shadow," she said.

Jack stared a time longer into her eyes before going on.

"I'm not a little boy."

"Oh, no?" She asked, raising a brow.

Jack grabbed for her and squeezed her shoulders, kissing her deeply. At first Wendy stared wide-eyed at him, but then she gave in to it and even shared in it. Their exchange was cut short, however, by the sound of a cell phone being turned on.

They turned to Marty, still in each other's arms. They saw him sitting on the ground with the green light of the cellphone lighting his face. He looked up at them, smiling.

"Did you find that in the backpack?" Jack asked.

119

"Yup." Marty grinned. "And it still has a little battery life left too."

"Sweet!" Jack said letting go of Wendy and walking to him.

"Does it have a signal?" Wendy asked enthusiastically.

"Uh, not yet," Marty said, looking at the cell phone screen. "I can't imagine it getting anything down here."

"So, we get out of here and then find a spot where we can make a call," Jack said, smiling.

"This phone is old. What are the odds that it still has service?" Marty asked, thinking it over.

"Oh, crap. I didn't think of that." Jack rubbed his face with his hands, thinking. Suddenly the cellphone beeped, and they all looked at it. "What was that?"

"For a second it got one bar," Marty said, smiling again. "Maybe we could finally be catching a break."

They looked over and saw Wendy tracing the walls again.

"Hey, does that help us getting out of here?" Jack asked.

Wendy ignored him and walked around the room. "Hey, take a look at this," she said, waving them over. "I think this tells a story of a kind of plague that devastated parts of what was ancient Egypt. This is very old. This could be one of the biggest finds in years … maybe centuries!" Wendy said, getting excited.

"Do dead people celebrate?" Jack asked sarcastically.

"The Egyptians believed they do."

"Well, that's great for them."

"Anyway…" Wendy went on. "If I'm reading this right it says this guy, Arakis, found this disease somewhere and started using it for … oh, man." Wendy stopped studying a piece of the wall.

"What?" Marty asked, getting up and looking at the hieroglyphics. "What did he do?"

CHAPTER 13

ARAKIS

Ancient Egypt

"Master Arakis?" the young man with a shaven head and black outlined eyes asked, bowing deeply inside the temple door. Arakis sat in a large stone chair, staring out at his garden that lay just beyond him through an opening surrounded by high white pillars. Two slave women, wearing little more than a veil, fanned him with large woven fans. Arakis was a muscular man for a priest. He had spent most of his life as a soldier until realizing the benefit of convincing people that he was blessed and should be spending the rest of his days as a priest of Thoth, the Moon-god of writing and science. He sat in his chair, frowning and tapping his chin with a thick finger that was well adorned with golden rings.

"Master Arakis?" the young man tried again. "The General has agreed to meet with you."

Arakis turned his way without saying a word.

The young man went on. "He is…" He paused, clearing his throat nervously. "-he is annoyed."

"Annoyed?" Arakis asked in his deep commanding voice. The man immediately looked back to the ground, and the slave girls picked up the pace of their fanning. "The General is weak." Arakis stood from his

122

chair and walked to the wall to look up at the statue versions of his god and many others. The area was lined with them and Arakis walked around, staring up at the faces of each until coming to Thoth.

"I will use this gift to smite the enemies of Egypt and help this great land become the place it should be. The place where all others bow to our might and superiority in *all* things." He frowned, turning back to the man waiting patiently, still bowing. "Bring the General here. Make sure no one disturbs us." Arakis waved him off. The young man bowed lower, respectfully, and left.

"Leave me," he said to the women kneeling by his chair. Arakis watched them leave and walked to a hanging tapestry of his god. Arakis took one more look around before moving the tapestry aside and opening a door that was hidden beyond it. Dim light from the burning lamps below lit the stone stairway as Arakis quickly descended. At the bottom, there was a large room with two dungeon-like cells and an altar with two tall lamps burning around it. Arakis stepped up to the altar, smiling. He looked over the body that lay there in amazement as he had many times before. It still wore pieces of the robes of a worshipper of Thoth. Other than that, however, there was nothing left to show who it had once been. The skin on the body was black with short coarse hair. The head was Jackal-like with yellow eyes staring up to the ceiling in death. It still had a snarl on its canine face, and Arakis thought even in death it was a personification of rage and madness.

He absently waved away the insects that fed on the corpse's flesh. He reached into a pocket and pulled out a golden cylinder with a curved claw ending to it. He put it on one finger and jammed it into the stomach of the corpse. He moved it around several times before pulling it free. He looked at the black blood on the tip, smiling before taking it off and returning it to his pocket.

"You have served me well," he said to the altar. "I am sorry that you had to find your end in this way, but know that in death you will be helping Egypt in a way you could have never done in life. To think this gift would be found in the midst of some lowly Nubian village. They worshipped and feared it, great Thoth, but I know why you have led my followers to it. What good is a sword without the hand that can wield it?" Arakis whirled, laughing, and headed for the stairs. He felt the bite of a mosquito and slapped his arm, brushing away the black blood it left behind absently as he took the stairs two at time.

As Arakis pulled aside the tapestry, he saw the General leaning against a pillar and staring out at the garden.

"The gods bless you, General," Arakis said, walking towards him.

"If they did, they would not have me here waiting for you and your nonsense," the General said, turning around and frowning deeply. The General was a tall thin man who looked as if he would have been better-suited to a life of eating exotic fruit out of the hands of pretty slave women rather than a life of a soldier. Arakis could not help noticing that the man had not a toned muscle on his body, and he thought there was most likely not a callous anywhere on him. This general commanded from the back of every battle, and the thought of it made Arakis want to strike the coward dead where he stood.

124

"Please, General." Arakis gestured towards the garden stones. "If you would walk with me so that I may tell you why I have asked for your audience."

"Let's make this quick, Arakis. I have real things to do."

Arakis bit his lip as he stepped into the garden with the General in tow.

Today you will do your first and most important duty for Egypt.

"Let's hear it, Arakis. Why am I here?"

"I feel that there is great change coming and I wonder where you will be when it comes?"

"Great change? Do not be cryptic with me. Some may believe that you have had some great calling, but I know you to be just the low-ranking front-line soldier you have always been. Do not waste my time, priest." He said the last with such disdain that Arakis had to take a moment to swallow so as to not to grab the man, snap his neck, and leave his weak body to feed his garden flowers.

"Then I will not waste another moment," Arakis said, reaching into his pocket and slipping his finger into the cylinder. He shot forward and grabbed the General's skinny arm.

"Let go of me!" the General yelled, trying to pull free from Arakis' iron grip.

"You will be the one that will prove to Pharaoh that Egypt now has the power to wipe out its enemies once and for all."

"I will do nothing of the sort. Arakis, I will have you skewered for this, you damn fool. LET ME GO!"

Arakis did and the General took several steps back, staring murderously at the priest. "I will have no part in your schemes. You are mad!" The General whirled around dramatically and stomped off. Arakis saw the satisfying small trickle of blood running down the back of his arm.

CHAPTER 14
SWALLOWING EGYPT

The Tomb of Arakis

"So, some priest dude started spreading some disease or something?" Marty asked, looking at the wall.

"They call it The Curse of Anubis," Wendy said, stepping to the next wall with her flashlight lighting the way. "Apparently, this Arakis guy meant to use it against the enemies of Egypt."

"You mean he was the first Saddam Hussein?" Jack asked, following her progress and holding the lantern for more light.

"Yeah, I guess," Wendy said chuckling. "Looks like this *dude* lost control of it and it started infecting Egyptians."

"Why does it look like that Jackal-headed dude actually eating someone?" Marty asked, studying one of the hieroglyphics.

"The Egyptians liked to depict things in pictures. I'm sure what they meant is that the diseased ravaged the people, represented by Anubis here eating them."

"Why Anubis?" Jack asked. "I thought he was a good guy that weighed the hearts of the dead before allowing them entrance into the duat underworld place?"

Wendy looked over at him with an impressed look on her face. "So, you did pay attention in at least one of those classes."

"It must have been in one of those mummy movies I watched or something," Jack shrugged.

"Well, it seems to me," Wendy went on, ignoring him, "that this Arakis thought the gods gave him this disease to help protect Egypt. He saw it as a weapon and planned to use it as such. But it looks like it spread and he got blamed for it. He thought he was going to be a great crusader for Egypt, and it seems he was killed and ... no way." She said, putting her nose closer to the wall.

"What?"

"I can't be reading this right."

"What do you think it says?" Jack asked, coming up beside her.

"This place must be even older than I thought." She blew at the symbols on the wall to remove some of the dust. "If this is right, and there may be another way to read this, it says here that they started the first mummifications not so the person could preserve their body in the afterlife but ... this doesn't make any sense."

"It's because they didn't want them to come back to swallow Egypt. It was to make sure they stayed dead," Marty said, as he followed them across the room.

Wendy and Jack turned towards him as he stared at the image of the Jackal- headed god swallowing a line of people in ancient Egyptian garb.

"Why would they do that?" Wendy asked confused. "You think it was superstition?"

"I think it was more than that," Marty went on. "Jack, you said you got a glimpse of those dog things out there. What did you see?"

"Dude, I didn't see a Jackal-like werewolf thing," he said back, angrily.

"What did you see? That's all I'm asking, man. You saw something. What was it?"

"Let's just drop it," Jack said, walking to where the packs were and picking them up. "We need to find a way out of here … now."

Marty and Wendy watched him closely without saying a word.

"What?" He asked defensively.

Wendy came up to stand in front of him. "What did you see, Jack?"

Jack rolled his eyes, sighing. "Come on guys. This is ridicuous. What do you want me to say? You want me to tell you I saw a huge animal run across the sand on all fours and then stand on two to look right at me. Is that what you want to hear? Then fine, that is what I saw. It was dark and it could have been anything."

Wendy looked at his hands holding the pack and saw them shaking.

Marty too came up close to Jack. "Something was attacking the men out there and it wasn't wild dogs, man. Whatever that was that looked through that tent the other night was no fucking wild dog, man. I know a fucking dog, man!"

What are we saying here boys?" Wendy asked, looking at them back and forth.

"Fine, if you ain't gonna say it, I will." Marty crossed his arms in front of him. "I don't think the Anubis Curse is only in hieroglyphics."

TOMB OF ARAKIS

Ancient Egypt

Arakis waited in his chair, staring at his now-unkempt garden. The statue of Thoth lay on the ground smashed to pieces. He had taken a regiment of the Pharaoh's soldiers and did what had to be done to the towns on the outskirts of the city. It was obvious now that his worshippers had not come straight to him after finding the ancient skull, as was his command to them. It seems they had visited their villages first to see their families. Now they and their families were dead. Arakis knew now why he could not find them weeks ago. They had obviously been turning, becoming what he had envisioned for the enemies of Egypt.

Arakis sighed and ran his hand across his tired eyes. As he did, he looked down at the bandage that surrounded his arm. It was soaked in pus and blood. The flesh around the bandage was turning black. He knew it was only a matter of time. He had no idea how he had become infected, but there was no denying that he was. The great weapon provided by the gods was being turned against him. Angrily, he looked over at the broken statue.

"Why do you smite me so?" he yelled.

"Master," the young priest said, stepping into the temple.

"What is it?"

"Soldiers are coming," the young man said, unable to keep his eyes off his master's arm. His hair had begun to grow back and the ink around his eyes was almost gone.

Arakis stood from his chair and came towards him. The young man took several steps back, unable to meet Arakis' eye. Arakis kept his distance, frowning.

"Go to the house and tell my family to get out. Tell them to leave everything and run. Do it now!"

"That will not be necessary," the General said, stepping into the clearing.

Arakis sighed, leaning against a post. "Too much to ask for a last meal?" Arakis meant it to be a feeble joke, but in truth was he was so hungry he was finding it hard to concentrate. Then the soldiers came into the clearing, trampling what was left of his garden.

"Bring them," the General commanded.

Several soldiers dragged his wife and three of his four kids into the temple. Arakis prayed to all the gods that the missing one had escaped.

"You have brought shame not only to your family but to all of Egypt," the General smiled viciously. Arakis wondered just how hard it would be to rip the man's head off his skinny neck with his bare hands.

"Hold him!" The General commanded. He took a deep look into Arakis' eyes. "Double up and hold him still!"

"Wherever I am going, General," Arakis smiled, "Know that you will be soon following. Look to your arm."

The General looked around his arm and found the spreading blackness growing there. "Bring the family and place them in front of him!"

"Be an honorable man and leave them out of this!" Arakis pleaded.

The soldiers brought his wife and children to the front and pushed them to their knees.

The General leaned in close to Arakis' ear. "Be an honorable *man*? It seems you have taken that from me already, haven't you? Know that your family will accompany you in your tomb. Buried alive ... or that is, mostly alive." The General grabbed Arakis' hair and pulled his head back. Arakis looked into his wife's eyes as she covered her children's. The general pulled his short sword free and ran it across Arakis' throat. Blood flew into the air and the General aimed the flow to fall on Arakis' family. With his dying strength he tried to pull away, but the soldiers held tight and he watched as his blood infected his family. The General leaned into his ear. "It seems the Pharaoh will not burn you as not to upset Thoth and his followers but know that we will take your body apart. And also know that your family will become that which you have brought to Mother

Egypt, in that tomb. Die Arakis ... go and be judged by that which has forsaken you."

The body of Arakis was dissected by priests that were careful to remove all organs to be sure he could not come back to life as the monster they had seen. They were taking no chances and used tools so as not to come in contact with the infection. Each part removed was put in jars and sealed. They then wrapped the body tightly in cloth that was dipped in a tar just to be sure that if he did rejuvenate, he could not get free. As a final precaution, they sealed the body in a heavy rock casket.

A small squad of soldiers and priests took the sarcophagus to a secluded place in the desert. It was night and torches lit the area. Several men in red robes and shaved heads exited the cave in the side of the hill. They held many paints and chiseling tools. Arakis' wife was shoved towards the cave, still clutching her children. A man silently came into the light area covered head to toe in cloth. He reached out with a gloved hand indicating for the soldiers to drag them into the cave.

The woman cried out for mercy for her children, but the General. deep in his cloth, heard none of it from beneath his hood. It was all he could do to fight the madness that struggled for control. He knew it was only a matter of time before it would win but he wanted to stay alive at least long enough to see Arakis and his family banished from this life ... and the afterlife. There was no telling why the gods had cursed him but with hope now that Arakis was to be judged the curse would be over. And with all the rights and respect for the gods, surely the curse would also be lifted from him and all others. The General fully expected that as the tomb was sealed he would have his body back.

"Get 'em in and close it!" he spat out in his now-deformed mouth. He heard a rider approaching and looked behind him from deep beneath his hood. Apprently no one else heard it as he was the only one to turn.

"Sir ... is something wrong?" a nearby soldier asked.

"You cannot hear that?" he hissed back, annoyed.

"I hear noth-" the soldier stopped as the rider trotted slowly into the clearing in the soft sand.

The soldiers snapped to attention, immediately saluting. The soldier nearest him raised his sword and it took all the General had not to devour the meaty muscled arm in front of him. He stared at it from beneath the hood, trying desperately to get the image of ripping the arm from the man's body out of his mind. He could, in his mind, feel the hot blood hit the roof his mouth and splash his face. From there he could-

"Hold there," the rider commanded the men hoisting the stone to seal the cave.

"What right!" the General growled. The sound of it was so fierce that everyone stared at him. The General shifted uneasily beneath the many robes, knowing even to his ears how vicious it had sounded.

"General," the rider said, trying to gain control of the horse as it tried to bolt. "I have a command from the Pharoh himself.

"Speak it then." The General heard rustling in the sands beyond them and knew that men were there hidden from view. "What are you planning?" He tried to push back the rage, but he knew that one more small thing and he would be lost to it.

"It is my honor to send you to Osiris, General. You will be missed." The rider's horse took several steps back and whinnied pathetically. "Please, General, try to…"

But the General was gone. What was left of him fell on his knees and bellowed in agony as the body twisted and turned underneath the robes. The people in the clearing watched and winced as they heard bones snapping underneath. Then, as quickly as it had begun, it ended. The pile of what looked to be only discarded robes started to rise. The men marveled as it rose to several heads higher than the General had just once been.

"SHOOT IT! SHOOT IT!" the rider said, waving his hands frantically as the horse reared. Two black clawed hands shot out from under the robes and ripped the rider off the horse, followed by a loud crunch and an enraged snarl. The horse reared again, eyes wide, and tried to bolt, but the creature lunged and bit deep into its neck. The horse screamed as it was pulled to the ground, blood shooting up to the heavens. The soldier that had come with the General could only stare at what was happening around him. He watched as the dark canine creature fed on the horse's flesh. It ripped off long chucks of horse and swallowed loudly. Finally, the head of the beast rose, and the man looked into the yellow madness of its eyes. Horse flesh and blood dripped from its long sharp-toothed maw.

"For Re's sake, shoot it!" he yelled out, falling to the sand. He pushed himself backwards slowly. The creature jumped into the air with another mad snarl. Arrows whistled through the air, knocking it wide from its target. It hit the ground with a thud.

"MORE! YOU IDIOTS!" the man called as the cursed beast that was once the General pulled itself on its side towards him. Its long red tongue licked its black lips as it tried to get to him by pulling itself with one sinewy arm. More arrows fell and the man watched as life left the thing but seeing even then that the madness seemed to remain.

Another man walked into the clearing from the darkness,"You there," the riderless man said to the soldiers in the clearing who were still staring, unable to move. "Take it and put it in the cave." He spat on the ground, looking at the dead beast. When he sensed no one moving, he glared at them. "Now! Move it!" The soldiers reluctantly came up and pulled what was once their General towards the cave. The woman peered out of the opening, looking around as if thinking of making an escape. She disappeared inside again as the soldiers heaved the creature inside. As soon as the soldiers were inside, the man waved to the others outside hiding in the darkness and they ran in, hoisting the large rock quickly to seal it. The soldiers inside screamed, trying to stop its fall, but it was no use. The door sealed with a rumble and a bang of finality.

"Cover it with sand," the man said, coming over to look at the dead horse. He then heard a familiar whistle in the air above him. He suddenly knew why the Pharaoh had chosen him, a low-ranking officer, to carry out his orders this day.

"May the curse find you too one day, Divine One." He swore bitterly as the arrows came down on him like rain.

CHAPTER 15
ESCAPE

"Werewolves?" Wendy asked crossing her arms and looking down at Marty critically. "Are you serious?"

"Is it so impossible?" Marty asked, lighting his joint again. The ancient pictures on the walls lit up from the flame, and then they were around the small light of the lantern again in almost utter darkness. "There have been stories of people turning into animals since forever. You said it yourselves."

"This is stupid," Jack interrupted. "We need to get the fuck out of here and not tell ghost stories."

"You can play the rational grounded one if you want but we need to know what we're into," Wendy chided.

"We're *into* a fucking cave, man!" Jack spread his arms turning. "You see? A real motherfucking dark ass cave with who knows how much air left in it! Can we please concentrate on the task at hand?"

Marty sucked in another drag from his joint. "And what might that be?"

Jack looked over at Wendy, shaking his head wonderingly. She wouldn't meet his eye but shook her head too, frustrated and confused.

"To get the hell out of here … what do you think?"

After an uncomfortable period of silence, they decided it was best to investigate the cave and perhaps find a way out that way. Wendy told them they had maybe a day's worth of battery in the lanterns, so they kept them dim and traveled by touch. Marty brought up the back and made small marks on the walls as he passed them with a lipstick he found in the intern's backpack. Wendy, of course, vehemently objected but finally gave in to the logic of it.

They had not gone far before they felt things crushing under their feet. Wendy cringed everytime something snapped. Jack knew what she was thinking. Priceless Egytian artifacts being destroyed with every step. He knew, however, that there was a real chance that if they didn't find a way out soon it could very well be their tomb, as well. Whatever Raul had brought them here for was spinning out of control outside this cave. The 'wild dogs' were attacking them and there was no telling if even Raul and Siam were still alive. For all he knew they were all dead and whatever was out there killing was right now looking for a way into the cave just as they were looking for a way out. The thought did nothing to lighten his mood or help motivate him into taking his next awkward step.

Something snapped under him, and he lost his footing. He reached out widely for something and grabbed Wendy's arm by accident. She too lost her footing and they both fell together to the floor. Jack's lantern flickered as it hit the ground and went out. Jack swore and Wendy groaned in pain.

"Are you all right?" he asked her, reaching out in the darkness.

Wendy at first didn't answer, but Jack heard her rubbing something as she tried to subdue the pain.

"Hey," Marty called out behind them. "You guys plan on turning that light back on?"

"Yeah, hold on a second." Jack looked for the 'on' button in the darkness. He found it and clicked a few times with no effect. "Shit!"

"Okay, don't move," Wendy said. "Touch the bottom of the lantern and see if the battery hatch is open."

Jack did and sure enough it was open. He touched inside and thankfully felt the battery. He sat up in the darkness and did a silent prayer closing the hatch. It immediately lit up. Jack looked to his left and yelled, pushing himself away from the gaping mouth of a large canine skull.

"Oh, shit man!" He held the lantern out at it as if it were a shield.

"It looks like they had trouble with wild dogs in here too," Marty said in a quiet voice.

"Hey," Wendy said in a shaky voice. "I think there's more over here." Jack stood and raised the lantern. Sure enough, there were bones scattered all around the room. A skull that looked to be a combination of the canine skull and a human's lay next to Wendy's leg as she sat staring at it.

"Is that-?"

"Marty, I will punch you right in the head if you say it," Jack said between clenched teeth. "Let's just find a way out of here, all right?"

"I may have a problem," Wendy said from the floor. They looked down and she was looking at her leg. Jack stepped closer, raising the light. They saw something poking out of her thigh.

"That yours or someone else's?" Marty asked.

"I think it someone else's."

"Oh, shit. What do we do?"

Jack came over to her side to get a better look. "That is totally gross."

"That's your expert opinion?" she asked.

"Sorry."

"-about what? Knocking me down or the fact that I now have a thousand-year-old person's bone stuck in my leg?"

"Both ... sorry."

"All right, now that that is taken care of, what do you suggest?" She leaned her head against the wall behind her, sighing. She opened her eyes, looking through her tears. She felt them roll down her cheeks and she saw something written above her in big letters. She turned her head sideways, but couldn't make it out. She looked over at Jack who was staring at the words with out saying a word. "What is it?" she asked at his blank face. "What is it?" She looked over at Marty who was looking at it in the same way. "Will someone please tell me what is going on?"

"It's a message," Jack said like in a trance. "It's from my father ... and it ain't good."

"Oh." Wendy swallowed hard, looking at them. "Can you ... can you tell me what it says."

"Yeah ... yeah all right. It says: they killed me. They killed us all. I am dead as I write this. The curse is real. If this gets out it could destroy us all. DO NOT LET IT OUT! It is signed Dr. John Edwards. I know the signature ... it's his."

"The curse is real?" Wendy asked, scooting around so she could see better. She hissed at the pain but was able to move. "If we read the walls right, the curse was some kind of disease."

"I thought we decided-"

Jack gave Marty a dangerous look.

"Dude." Marty nodded towards a corner of the room. Jack took his time turning with the light not sure he wanted to see what was there. When he finally did see he wished he hadn't. There were several bodies piled up and decomposing. Some were obviously partially consumed. They heard a distant howl. They listened silently until it ended.

"Please tell me that was outside the cave," Marty said, in a shaking voice.

CHAPTER 16
THE PLAN

"That I had not planned on," Khalid said into the phone as he sat in his elaborate office inside the mountainside. He absently played with a tassel on the lamp shade with the toe of his boots and leaned back in his big leather chair, his feet on the desk. "The one we serve has … dramatic goals that may lack in reality in some small way." He reached over and pulled a lit cigarette from the ashtray, listening half-heartedly to whoever was speaking on the other side. "Listen to me. I do not carry which one gets the curse." Again, Khalid listened, rolling his eyes as he watched the smoke rise up to the ceiling. "Okay, I don't mean to be insulting, my friend. It is just that we could get the same effect if any one of them were to bring the curse back with them. I know M…" Khalid held the phone from his ear as someone on the other end yelled.

"Yes-yes. I was not going to say his name. As I was going to say. I know *he* would like it to be the son of the pillaging westerner, but we have to face the fact that it is more important to finish the ultimate goal of the mission than to … was that gunfire?" Khalid took his feet off the desk and leaned forward on the phone.

"They cannot all die … we need one of them … what are you saying?" Khalid stood, his eyes wide. "You mean to tell me that you have seen one of them?" Khalid held the phone from his ear, cringing from the gun shots on the otherside. "Please tell me that that is not what you're shooting at … how many?"

144

Khalid fell back into his chair, pulling his cigarette from the ashtray with a now shaking hand. "Destroy them completely ... if any get beyond the desert ... be sure of that." Khalid reached into his drawer and pulled out a bottle of pills. "No, the one I was sending you has not even arrived yet." Khalid held the phone away from his ear again as the person on the other end yelled. "Yes, I know what that means. That is what I was telling you. The ones you have seen are not related to the one I'm sending." Khalid poured a handful of pills into his hand and shoved them into his mouth. "I will have that one destroyed," Khalid said, as he spat one of the pills across the room. "For fuck's sake, find out where they're coming from...Yes, and get one of them on the plane back to their home. Yes, I think you should destroy all but one of them ... fine, fine if it's the son then fine. I don't care, just make sure you kill everything there before leaving ... yes, EVERYTHING!" Khalid hit the button on the phone and threw it as if it was itself infected. "The idiots. They'll kill us all!" Khalid opened his desk drawer, looked to make sure no one was looking, and pulled out a bottle of whiskey that he immediately put to his lips.

CHAPTER 17
REAL RAUL

Raul closed his cell phone, looking around. The creatures had stopped coming at them and the men were busying themselves with setting the dead aflame ... beast and human. He knew there was no reason to take any chances. He heard someone screaming nearby and saw that one of the victims was not quite dead. Raul walked up to the flames and fired his pistol twice into it. The screaming stopped, the man's head fell to one side, and Raul saw that it was his driver. He grunted miserably, putting his gun in its holster inside his jacket. The next thing he knew, something crashed into his side and he was rolling down the sand embankment. Every time he rolled; he saw a dark figure coming closer to him. He reached for his gun and pulled it out as he rolled. At the bottom of the hill, he raised his gun, but it was on top of him. He reached out with his left hand grabbing at its throat. Raul was slammed onto his back. He held it away from his face as he tried to aim the gun. The big mouth snapped in Raul's ear as he pushed with everything he had to keep it off of him. There was a gunshot and the thing grunted and looked away for second. It was all Raul needed to get his aim and fire. The shot knocked it to its side and Raul rolled over and stood. The creature lunged from the ground, but Raul kept firing into its canine head until it stopped moving.

Raul looked over his shoulder at the young soldier who held the gun that had saved his life.

"Have you been wounded by it?" Raul yelled to him.

"N-no, sir," the soldier said, pulling his robe over to one side. From where he stood, he could see the small stain of blood that he was trying to hide. Raul raised his gun.

"NO! It's not from the-"

Raul shot the man in the head.

"Thank you for saving me," Raul said, watching the soldier fall onto his back on the sand.

CHAPTER 18
PAN TO THE FIRE

"You volunteer in an ER every week?" Jack asked Marty, skeptically. "Get out of here."

Marty shrugged, going through the intern's bag again.

"That can't true." Jack went on shaking his head at him. "You were playing Dungeons and Dragons ... that's where you're going."

"Dude, I haven't played Dungeons and Dragons since I was in high school. And if I remember correctly, Mr. Druid half-elf, I wasn't the only one."

Jack looked over at Wendy and she raised her hands in the air, nodding to her wounded leg as if to say, 'what the hell?'

"Oh, sorry," he said shrugging. "Um, so what do you think ... doc?"

"I think if I can find what I'm looking for and if that bone didn't hit an artery, we'll be on our way."

"Hate to interrupt you two *dorks*.," Wendy interrupted. "But how about you share some of that insight with me ... you know ... the patient."

Marty looked up and smiled. It was such a disarming smile that Wendy thought to herself that she really did like him. His smoking and white boy dreadlocks aside, of course.

"I have been volunteering at the ER," Marty said, rummaging again in the pack. "And I am third in my class for pre-med."

"No way," Wendy said, legitimately bewildered.

"Oh, way." Marty answered. "Ah, Ha!" he said elatedly.

"What are you looking for?" she asked him, suspiciously.

Marty held up a small tube, smiling. Wendy read the label.

"Crazy glue? You were looking for crazy glue?"

"Yup."

"And may I inquire as to why?"

"Sure." He smiled.

"Okay … why?" she asked, feeling a little nauseous.

"I'm going to pull that thing out of you and then glue the hole closed."

"The hell you are!"

Jack laughed bitterly at him. "You've smoked yourself stupid, dude."

"Listen." Marty let the smile wash away from his face. "We have no idea when we're going to find a hospital. And unless you want to walk around with that thing in ya, for God knows how long, we need to get it out and stop the bleeding. Now I can do this. Doctors are actually using something pretty close to this now in hospitals, so let's say we stop running our gums about it and get this done so we can find a way out of here and back to our lives, huh?"

Wendy rubbed her eyes with her hands. "Oh, shit ... shit ... SHIT!"

"What you want me to do, doc?" Jack asked putting the lantern down and coming up beside them.

"Give her your wallet to bite down on."

Jack pulled his wallet from his back pocket. Wendy looked at it dubiously. "I ain't putting something in my mouth that's been on your ass for God knows how-"

"Wendy, take it and get ready now," Marty said seriously, ripping her pants leg. Wendy bit down and whimpered. "Jack, hold her leg still. I need to do this fast so hold tight."

Wendy looked at Jack and he tried to smile encouragingly. He felt a rush of guilt wash over him seeing her so scared.

"I'm so sorry," he said honestly. Then her eyes went huge, and she screamed through her clenched teeth as Marty ripped the bone free. Jack looked away, unable to watch. Wendy screamed again as Marty held the wound closed.

"Hang in there ... almost done," he said, working quickly.

"That was really awesome ... seriously." Jack smiled, shaking his head in wonderment.

"Thanks, man," Marty said cheerfully, pulling something from the pack and stuffing it in his mouth. "Something about doctoring makes me famished!"

"What is that?"

"Not sure. I found it in the intern's pack." Marty shrugged, "tell you the truth, I don't care. I got to get something in my stomach."

Jack laughed at him and put his hand on Wendy's shoulder. "You coming back to us?" Wendy opened her eyes a little and nodded. "Okay, good. I think we should probably start looking for a way out again." Wendy nodded again and offered her hand to help her up. Jack stood and slowly pulled her to her feet. Wendy winced the whole way but came up. "Good. Now, can you put weight on it?" Wendy tried and found she could, slightly. "All right, lean on me and Marty can take the lead."

"Me?"

"Dude, come on. You just pulled that whole doctor crap out of your ass ... now we need a cave guide. Do your stuff." Jack handed him the lantern and Marty led the way reluctantly.

"Hey," Wendy said leaning on Jack. "Do you think we're gonna ... you know ... get out of here?"

"Yeah, we'll make it." Jack tried very hard to keep the confidence in his voice.

"He said he was dead already. What do you think he meant?"

"I don't know. But for right now, let's just concentrate on getting out of here."

"Maybe it's safer in here."

"It is for now. But if we stay, we'll run out of air, or starve, or Raul and his buddies will come in here looking for us. I think we have a better chance on our own."

"I think I saw one of those things, too."

Jack looked down at her as they walked, following Marty's light. "I admit this makes no sense. I mean, come on … there's no way … but … well you saw. Can there really be such a thing?"

"I'm a scientist." Wendy shook her head. "There has to be a logical explanation."

Suddenly a sharp beeping sound filled the cave.

"What was that?" Jack called up to Marty.

"That, my friends, was one bar," Marty called back cheerfully.

"You got a signal?" Wendy asked excitedly.

"Yup … it's gone but-" Marty was interrupted by another beep. "There's got to be a cell tower around!"

"Move it around to find out where it's getting the signal," Jack offered.

"Dude, who you gonna call?"

"No one! It will tell us which way is out."

"Oh." Marty thought for a second, looking at the cave walls. "Because it will most likely have a signal where the walls are thinnest … or there is an opening."

"Duh," Jack replied.

Marty moved the phone up and down and around the opening in the cave. He walked over and ran it down a rock piled on one side. The phone beeped again. Marty held still and looked into the phone without moving. "It's holding the signal right here."

"Then let's start digging."

"Alright, get them out of there," Raul said, brushing the dust off his suit. "And bring one of those things unburned."

"Sir, you want one of those things?" A soldier in desert fatigues asked, looking over at the dead creature lying in the sand near him.

"Bring the thing here." Raul pointed to a spot in front of him angrily. "Slit the thing open from groin to chest. Then get Dr. Edwards' son and bring him here." Raul pointed to another place in the sand.

Siam came up the hill to stand next to Raul. "What do you plan to do?" he asked, putting his gun in the holster at his side.

"What I do is of no concern of yours." Raul put his large nose in the air indignantly. He saw Siam's obvious discomfort and decided to add to it. "I am going to rub the thieving doctor's son's nose right into the beast's belly. That's what I'm going to do. Too much was left to chance and it's time to get this plan going. It is time to bring death to the westerners as they have brought it to us for so many years." Raul spat on the ground, disgusted.

Siam sighed and rubbed his chubby fingers across his face. "Can you tell me? Are my children well? Is Donya taking her medicine and is Predish not picking on his little sister? "

Raul looked at him, smirking. "Do not worry about your children. Your job is clear, and it is your duty to Allahh that you perform it. Remember who and what you are, Siam."

"I know who I am." Siam tried to keep the tears from his eyes. He had been around Raul's kind long enough to know from the smirk that they were already dead. "I will bring you the boy," he said, and marched towards the cave. Tears streamed down his face as he walked.

My sweet ones, please forgive me.

Wendy could only watch now, as it was too much for her to keep bending and hoisting the rocks with her wound. She thought about investigating the writings on the walls again, but decided that at this point she really didn't want to know anymore. She was in a nightmare and she could not get out. If it wasn't for the all too real throbbing in her thigh, she would be sure it was just a bad dream. She wondered, as she watched the boys tossing the rocks, if she was still young enough to start another life if she made it out. She liked numbers. Numbers were safe … and clean … and didn't try to eat anyone. Yes, she decided. Perhaps accounting was the place for her. She was sure that was something she could do.

"I think I see light!" Marty said, leaning into a hole that was behind the rocks. "It's up a bit, but I see it!"

Perhaps she could start a family. She was still young enough for that, and more than one man gave her looks so she knew she must be desirable to them. Maybe she could learn to love someone. Maybe someone other than the late Dr. Edwards. Maybe she would meet another safe accountant. Perhaps someone she could talk to about balance sheets and return on investments. Someone that came home every night. Someone that kissed her hello and goodbye each day. They would drive a safe Volvo and get life insurance. Maybe get a dog … maybe not a dog. A cat.

"Wendy!"

"Yeah, what?" she asked, looking up. Jack and Marty were staring at her. "What?"

155

"Are you ready?" Jack asked, looking at her concerned.

"Yeah, I'm ready," she said back defensively. "For what?"

They exchanged a glance and looked at her again, worriedly. "We're going to climb through this hole and see what's on the other side."

"I'll wait here."

"The hell you will," Jack said climbing beside her. "We stay together no matter what. I'm not leaving you."

Wendy looked into his eyes. Jack grabbed her hands in his and squeezed them reassuringly.

I wonder how he is with numbers.

She shook her head, clearing it.

"Wendy, are you alright?"

"Yes, yes. I can do it. Let's just go."

"Okay." Jack stood and pulled her up.

Jack led the way, then Wendy, and finally Marty. All crawling in the small, confined space that they had cleared.

Wendy was coming along slowly and swearing every time she pulled herself forward. Marty had said that the glue would keep her wound closed but she was still worried it could burst open at any time. Not to mention all the sharp stones underneath that stabbed at her at every

156

angle. The good news was that she did see light up ahead and that helped lighten her spirits … a bit.

"Okay." Jack stopped and looked back at them in the small space. "I'll go the rest of the way and see what's up there."

"Let me know if you see a McDonald's. I'm starving!" Marty said in the near darkness.

"Chicken nuggets with honey mustard sounds really good," Wendy said, trying to get comfortable in the small space.

"I could eat like ten Whoppers all by myself!" Marty answered wistfully.

"That's Burger King, douche bag," Jack said crawling away, but then he stopped and turned back. "Oh … sorry," he said to Wendy, realizing what he had just said.

Wendy laughed. "Yeah, because that's the worst thing you ever said, right?" Jack laughed nervously and continued on.

They watched him as he slowly climbed up ahead. They talked about some other fast food favorites. Both their stomachs started growling and they laughed.

"You ever have an In-and-Out burger?" Marty asked, wiping drool from his chin.

"Are you kidding? I love In-and-Out!"

Wendy looked up the hole and saw Jack making his way back. She mentally started preparing herself for the pain of moving again.

"There's a drive-thru up there?" Marty asked as Jack crawled up.

"We need to get going."

Wendy started, but Jack put a hand out to stop her. "No ... back."

"Back? Why back? We can't-" She was cut off when the light in the hole suddenly became significantly dimmer. She looked around Jack and saw something dark filling the hole where it let in the light. They all watched silently. They couldn't make out what it was but heard a double intake of breath and then an animalistic grunt.

"Go!" Jack pushed her. Wendy suddenly forgot about the pain in her leg and pulled herself as quickly as she could the way she came. Marty moved even quicker in front of her. A howl of rage from behind them filled the space, echoing off the rock. Jack chanced a look back and saw the dark thing struggling frantically to fit into the hole that led to the outside world. He was able to make out the long black arms and claws as it struggled to pull itself in. He turned back and moved as fast as he could in the tight space. He saw Wendy was already out and he moved fast, following her. He heard what sounded like it crawling inside. His heart was pounding and he felt lightheaded with fear. He rolled out of the hole and started throwing the rocks back in. He realized Wendy and Marty were not next to him and he looked around.

"COME ON, HELP ME!" he yelled.

No response.

He realized he couldn't fill the hole himself and started to panic. He fumbled at the holster that held the gun and pulled it out. He could now hear the breathing of the thing as it was almost through to them. "HEY!" He yelled, trying to get his companions' attention and held the gun up with shaking hands. He sensed movement to his side and chanced a quick glance. Wendy and Marty were backing up towards him. "IT'S COMING!" he yelled, trying to hold the gun steady. Then a giant dark canine head poked out, looking up at him. The long straight ears looked almost ridiculous on top of its head. Jack froze in terrified shock meeting the yellow eyes. He knew he had to pull the trigger, but his hands wouldn't work. It pulled itself out with big claws gripping the edge the of the hole and slowly stood, knowing that he had him. Jack followed the eyes up to the cave ceiling.

It was taller than a normal man and stood on what looked to be both animalistic and human legs only bent the wrong way like it would sprint at him at any moment. Jack took it all in from toe to nose. Its body was black, sinewy, and coated with fine black hair. He saw the thin muscular chest heave in and out as it took in the air of the cave. It opened its long protruding mouth with many sharp teeth and snarled down at him almost in a cruel human fashion.

When Jack once again got to the eyes, he took a half step back. They were yellow, wide and full of a madness that he had never thought possible. He felt that everything was wrong with this thing, and he needed to kill it. It should not exist, and he knew the world would be a better and safer place without this monster in it. He pulled the trigger. Nothing happened. He pulled again twice, but the trigger would not budge. He saw the thing lean back on its legs, ready to lunge. Jack squeezed his eyes shut, preparing for the worst.

Gunfire filled the cave. He heard Wendy's voice, but it sounded very far away. His ears rang from the loud noise in such a confined area, and he smelled the burned sulfur in the air but still he held his eyes shut. He felt it touch his shoulder and tried the trigger again and again.

"Jack ... it's alright." It was Wendy's voice again. But he was afraid of what he would find if he opened his eyes. What if he was imagining the gunshots and Wendy's voice? What if he opened his eyes and just saw the horrible creature ripping him apart and eating his flesh?

"Jack, open your eyes right now." He heard Siam's voice commanding him. Jack slowly did so and saw a bloody wall across from him. He realized he was still pointing the gun at the very same spot.

"Did I..."

"You were forgetting the safety, my friend," Siam said from behind him. Siam came close and pushed the gun down and Jack suddenly realized how tired his arms were.

"That's it, my boy," Siam said soothingly.

It was then that Jack noticed for the first time the dead creature at his feet. He yelled and jumped back.

160

"It's real, man … it's really fucking real!" Marty said, coming to stand next to Jack. "How could this be? I mean, this changes everything! I mean, does this mean that Casper the friendly ghost is going to fly out of his ass?" Marty jabbed a finger over to indicate Siam. "I mean this is fu-ucked up!"

"I do not know this Casper," Siam said from behind them. "But I do know that it is not advised to get to close to these things … even when they are expired."

Jack and Marty took another step back as one. Jack nearly tripped over Wendy. She winced and touched her leg.

"Sorry," Jack offered lamely, not realizing she was so close.

Siam cleared his throat to get their attention. They turned to him, and he put his gun in his holster. "We need to leave this place," he said simply.

"Really?" Marty put in sarcastically.

"Lead the way," Jack said, now feeling very tired. He dramatically indicated for Siam to start going the way they had come.

"No … we go back through there," Siam said, frowning.

"What!" Wendy held up her hands. "No way." Jack turned to her and for the first time saw the tears in her eyes. "No way am I going back in there. No God damn way!"

"Why back? What's wrong with the front door?" Jack asked, starting to feel his hands shake again.

Siam sighed and glanced back where he had come from before speaking. "There is only certain death that way. If we go through the hole, we may have a chance."

"What if there are more of those things through there?"

"If we go back then you all are dead. The only chance is through that hole, "Siam said the last with finality.

"How about you tell us what the hell is going on here, Elvis?"

"I will tell you everything, my friends. But right now, we need to get out of here. I will go first and kill anything that is on the other side. You must follow me, quickly. Our time is short. We may already be too late. Follow me now!" Siam dove into the hole and they heard him climbing quickly away.

Jack looked down again at the beast. Blood was pooling around it. "I think I'm ready to go home now."

"What do we do?" Wendy asked.

"He could be playing us again," Marty said.

Jack ran his hands through his hair and sighed. He looked back the way Siam had come and weighed his options. He then heard some of the soldiers' voices as they made their way towards them.

"This sucks," he said finally. "Okay ... get in there and follow Elvis."

He heard Wendy swallowing hard. "Marty first, then you, and I will go last. Elvis can shoot what's coming at us and I'll shoot what's behind us. FUCK!"

"Remember the safety," Marty said as he climbed into the hole. Jack would have retorted if he didn't feel so tired. Wendy silently picked up the lantern and climbed in. Jack pulled his gun free and followed.

They found Siam on the other side with his gun out, searching the large cave opening. There was another entrance of the cave opposite them that was small but let in a lot of light from the desert sun. There were mounds of clothes littered everywhere with partially eaten bodies inside them. Some of them looked new and wore soldier's uniforms.

"Oh, my God," Wendy said, holding her stomach as she looked around. "This can't be real."

"Let's get the hell out of here." Jack headed for the hole letting in the light.

"Hold," Siam said, running forward to go first. "They can be crafty." He slowly stuck his head out and was pulled out, legs flaring. An instant later, a creature's black head came in and looked them over one by one in the near darkness, as the creature's head blocked the light. This only made the creature's eyes glow, reflecting the light and looking even more dangerous. They heard gunshots outside the cave. Then it pulled itself the rest of the way in and stood. Jack, Marty, and Wendy

163

instinctively moved closer together. It snarled and then gunfire exploded from the hole that they came through. The creature jerked back and forth as the bullets hit it and then collapsed to the ground, convulsing as dark blood shot from its mouth. They turned and saw the soldier stepping out behind them. Then more gunfire and the soldier jerked back and collapsed. They turned and saw Siam halfway inside the cave again.

"Let's go!" He waved to them to hurry. They ran forward and followed Siam outside. The sun was so bright that they were temporarily blinded. "There is a small village not far from here. We will move fast, so keep up." Siam started jogging off. As he did, Jack saw the long blood-stained gashes on Siam's military jacket.

"I don't think I can make it," Wendy said breathlessly. Jack looked down and saw fresh blood around her wound. He took off his pack and dropped it to the ground.

"Climb aboard," he said, giving her his back.

"It'll be too much for you," she complained. He looked into her blue eyes and saw the pain there.

"Look, I am the leader here and I say get on my back. You let me worry about what's too much for me, alright?"

"You-"

"Shut up and come on!" he yelled at her. "We're all going to make it." He turned his back to her again. "Let's go ... move it." He was

164

thankful when he felt her pressed against him. He hoisted her up and made a quick walk following Marty and Siam's footsteps in the sand.

Over an hour later a village came into sight. The sun was on the way down and they were all thankful that they wouldn't be out in the desert alone in the night.

"It's not exactly a metropolis," Marty said, holding up his dreadlocks to air out his neck. The small buildings were dull and almost completely blended in with the sand. There was a dirt road that led between the houses and a slightly larger building in the center. Other huts littered the area around the road. Large birds circled overhead but, other than that, there was no visible living thing around.

"Where is … everyone?" Jack asked breathlessly from the sand dune overlooking the town. He put Wendy down and went to his knees to rest.

"Maybe there's a flying carpet festival next town over," Marty suggested, smiling. He looked over at Siam's angry face and took a more serious demeanor and clearing his throat, said, "Uh, sorry."

"Let us cautiously enter and look for a working vehicle," he said, walking towards the town without another word. Jack got up and punched Marty in the arm.

"What!?"

"Don't be a dick." Jack shook his head, disgusted.

He looked over at Wendy who was sitting in the sand trying to get comfortable. "You ready?" He asked her. She just groaned and struggled to get up. Jack grabbed her arm and helped her up.

"I could really use some water," she croaked. Jack looked at her leg and saw that there was still wet blood there. He knew he had to get her to a hospital soon.

"And some food," Marty said, also looking at Wendy's wound. "They have to have something there to eat, man. I'm starving!"

"Alright, let's go see what's waiting for us down there," Jack said, watching Siam as he was already cautiously walking up the road to the town with his gun in his hand.

They walked warily to the town, finding it easier to step on the hard-packed earth of the road. The sand had slowed them significantly and they were thankful that it was uneventful around them. The nothingness gave them a good vantage of what was coming in all directions. They used their ears more than their eyes and stared at the ground, concentrating on putting one foot in front of the other, with the town getting closer with every step. There was also a coolness in the air as the sun started its descent. Other than an occasional jet passing far above them there were no other human sounds.

They stood in the middle of the town looking everywhere for any sign of life. There was nothing but the birds overhead. A bucket hung by a well and it gently knocked the stone in a rare moment of a breeze. Other than that, there was no sound, no people, nothing to inidicate that there was any life left in the small town.

"There ain't going to be a car here, man," Marty said miserably, turning around and taking it all in. "And I ain't too fond of the thought of staying here for the night." He started for one of the huts.

"Hey, where you going?" Jack asked.

"I'm going to see if I can find some old Taco Bell or something," Marty said, disappearing through the doorway of a hut. Wendy headed for the bucket to get some water.

"Stay together," Siam called over his shoulder and headed for the bigger building.

"Where are you going?" Jack asked.

"I am going to look for something to help us get out of here, Mr. Edwards."

"We still need to have that talk, Elvis!" Jack yelled back at him. Siam ignored him and continued walking. "Yeah, just walk away." Jack yelled after him. "Because it's not like we're in the middle of nowhere in a dead town with a thousand-year-old curse meeting hairy beasts that want to eat us or anything."

"I would think more like over three thousand years old," Wendy said, sending the small red plastic bucket down into the well on the rope.

"Oh, well then," Jack said, throwing up his hands. "I wouldn't want to get the timeline wrong."

"Really, this is a most important Egyptological finding." Wendy went on ignoring him. "If the things in that cave are authentic, then everything we thought about mummification is ... well wrong." She pulled the bucket up and was elated at the clear water there. She gingerly put her lips in the water and sucked it in. Several minutes later, she wiped her mouth and leaned against the rocks of the well. "Just think of it," she said eenthusiastically. "We could change everything that was previously thought about the process and the rituals behind it!"

"You mean the whole mummy thing comes from not wanting the people to become wolf men after they're dead?" Jack asked, coming to take a drink of the water.

"Well, I wouldn't have put it that way," Wendy said, frowning. "But just think about it. It makes sense. I mean the Jackal-headed Anubis is said to be the one that brought Osiris back to life using his magic. The story is that Anubis used mummification then for the first time. People believed that it was meant to help preserve the body in the afterlife, but what if it was really used many years before that to make sure the body stays ... you know."

"Dead."

"Yeah." Wendy shrugged. "I mean they took out all the organs and wrapped the body just to make sure. Then, as time went by, the ritual was changed from making sure the person stays dead to the person gets to keep it in the afterlife." Wendy looked up at the sky, thinking. "This could change so many theories and explain a lot of mysteries."

"Like what?"

"It is said that at one point Ra had used Bastet, the cat-headed god, as his tool of vengeance. Perhaps there was a time when an animalistic creature did represent an Ancient Egyptian god ... and what if this is where those stories began."

"But it's a canine kind of thing."

"It doesn't matter. We're talking about thousands of years here." Wendy smiled and crossed her arms. Jack couldn't help but notice how much she seemed to like talking about this. "You know how in high school something would happen and you would hear about it and every time you did the story got a little bit more befuddled?"

"Befuddled?"

"Yeah, like the story would keep changing. Not a lot at first but after about a month it would be complete fiction. Well, imagine two or three thousand years go by. And imagine a society of people that feared Jackals."

"Why did they fear jackals?"

"Jackals were known to dig up the dead and eat them. So, they got associated with the dead ... or maybe the story of these things happened even longer ago and-" Wendy smiled. "See what I mean!" She laughed. Jack looked at her like she was crazy. "This could explain a lot."

"But it's all theory."

"Everything in archaeology is theory. I mean nobody was there to confirm or deny what happened." She shrugged. "That's what makes it fun. You have to figure it out."

"What's fun?" Marty asked, walking towards them eating something that looked dry and hard.

"Did you find anything?" Jack asked him.

"Just more dead things." He took a bite.

"People?" Wendy asked, wide-eyed.

Marty shrugged. "I think so."

Jack and Wendy exchanged a worried glance. "Are you with us?" Jack snapped his fingers.

"What?"

"You just told us that you may have seen a bunch of dead people and your munching on God knows what. Are you alright?"

"I actually feel better now that I have something to eat."

Alright, whatever." Jack shook his head, eyes wide. "Let's get to that building and see what Elvis has found." Marty froze, staring up the road. "What is it?"

"Someone's coming."

"Who?" Jack asked, straining his eyes to look down the road. "It's not the-"

"No." Marty interrupted. "It's more soldiers. Their walking … no … running."

"Running?"

Marty held his hand up for quiet before answering. "Those things are behind them."

"What!" Wendy stood up on her one good leg.

Marty looked at them. "We should go."

Jack put Wendy on his back, and they ran for the building. It was open and Jack tried to close the door but it was ripped off the hinges and smashed to bits on the floor. They ran up the stairs to the second floor. They found an office that still had a door and opened it. Siam sat behind a desk with his gun pointed at Jack's head. There was a bottle and a glass in front of him.

"Happy hour?" Marty asked, laughing. Jack looked at him sideways, unsure why his friend was acting so strange.

"Come in and close the door," Siam said, lowering the gun. He poured the contents of the bottle into a glass and drained it.

"They're coming," Jack said, going to the windows.

"It was just a matter time," Siam said, pouring himself another. "Be thankful the others aren't here yet."

"They're right behind them," Marty said, ripping another bite of whatever he had and chewing.

Siam leaned forward, looking Marty over. "And how would it be that you would know that?" he asked, furrowing his brow. Marty shrugged, saying nothing. Siam pulled his gun and pointed it at Marty's head.

"WHOA! WHOA!" Jack stepped in front of Marty with his hands up.

"I know he means something to you Mr. Edwards … but he's dead already."

"The hell he is!" Marty yelled, holding his hands up.

Siam said nothing but eventually lowered his gun, sighing.

"I think it's time to tell us what's going on here," Jack said, slowly putting his hands down as well. "Why are we here, Elvis?"

Marty went to the window, seemingly unperturbed by almost being shot in the head and looked outside. "-probably should make it short," he added in a bored tone.

Jack stared at Marty a second before turning back to Siam.

"Alright, why?"

"Well since I'm also already dead," Siam said, lifting the bottle to his lips and forgetting the glass all together.

"Please will you stop saying that?" Wendy said from the corner. "And by the way, we saw those words written in the tomb by Dr. Edwards." Siam nodded, acknowledging her sadly.

"Please, Siam?" Jack asked, sitting in a chair across from the metal desk where Siam was sitting. The sun was almost down, and half of Siam's face was hidden in shadow from the window in the corner that Marty calmly looked through. The aging Egyptian reached out and absently played with the label on the whiskey bottle.

"Your father has many men that ... are not appreciative of his work here. Some are very jealous of his success with his finds."

"This is about a jealous Egyptologist?" Jack asked, confused.

Siam shook his head before draining the glass again. "This is about hate that goes far beyond that for your father. They see Dr. Edwards as just another representation of all the things that the people I work for-

" Siam stopped and sighed as he leaned back into his chair. "-that is did work for, hate about westerners."

"So, this is political?"

"I believe it is more like social, or for some, perhaps psychological, my friend. Dr. Edwards had money, respect, women, and these people believe he had it all because of what he, in their opinion, had stolen from Egypt."

"Except the women," Jack added.

Siam chuckled, covering his big belly. "Yes, my boy. Those he brought with him." He winked at Wendy.

Wendy, at that moment, was sure that she hated this man. She imagined how nice it would feel to punch the big man in the face as she averted her eyes.

"So, what has that to do with me?" Jack asked, spreading his arms.

"You see, my boy, here-" Siam dramatically spread his arms indicating everything around him. "-father and son are the same. The sins of the father are the sins of the sons." Siam reached for the bottle again, but Jack grabbed it first. He pulled the cork out and took a deep drink. After rushing air between his lips, he handed the bottle back to Siam.

"As I was saying," Siam went on. "You are to be used as a carrier of a new biological weapon. My employer insisted that you be infected

174

by one of the creatures and then flown back to the U.S. He wanted you to find the tomb of Arakis first and then be sent home ... with it."

"A biological weapon?" Jack asked, eyes wide. He looked over at Wendy and knew she was thinking the same thing. "Like what happened in Egypt in those cave pictures?"

Siam looked at him, impressed. Jack saw it and shook his head. "Not me," he said, nodding to Wendy. "She figured it out."

Wendy stepped up to the desk and for the first time noticed the dark pool under Siam's chair. "So, the whole thing was a ruse to get Jack here?" she asked. Siam nodded. "Then what does all this have to do with me?"

"You have experience in these things and..." Siam paused, rubbing his face uncomfortably.

"What?" Wendy asked, looking at him dangerously.

"You were originally to come to the school to meet Jack."

"Yeah, I missed the plane. There was a seminar on ... wait a minute. Are you telling me I was ... the bait to get him here?" She shook her head as realization dawned on her. "This whole time I was just the piece of ass to entice him?" Wendy walked back to the wall, disgusted. "Oh, that's just great."

"Hey at least you weren't chosen to be the carrier of some ancient Sars virus that makes you into some B-movie killer monster."

"Why did you say I was dead already?" Marty asked from beside the window. They all turned to look at him. He turned away from the window to face Siam. Siam looked at him sadly. "I believe you show signs of being infected."

"I haven't been bitten as far I know."

"Any contact will do it."

"I have had no contact."

"Are you hungry?"

"What does that have to do with anything?" Marty said back angrily. "I'm always hungry ... even before coming to this hell hole!" He lashed out, pushing at a large file cabinet that stood beside him. The cabinet lifted into the air and crashed into a wall on the other side of the room. The others stared at it not saying a word. They knew even if the cabinet was empty it would have been a show of strength to even drag it across the room, not have it fly across as if it weighed nothing at all.

"Oh, shit man," Marty said, staring at the crumbled cabinet, eyes wide with disbelief.

"Dude, we'll get you to the hospital," Jack said, trying to sound comforting. BANG. A gunshot exploded in the room making them all jump. Gun smoke was everywhere, thickest around the now empty desk. Jack went quickly around, finding Siam on the floor in a pool of blood. One side of his head was blown apart. Jack looked over and saw the smoking gun still in Siam's hand.

"He killed himself," Jack said in disbelief. "He just fucking killed himself!"

"Look at his side," Wendy said, coming up next to him and pointing. There were two long bleeding gashes soaking his clothes. "He must have thought he was infected." As the realization hit them, they turned together to Marty who was staring out the window again. "They heard that," he said calmly, turning to them. "My canine cousins are on their way here."

CHAPTER 19
THE HUNT

The building was in the center of the small town. It was not very large, maybe three stories, and held a few offices. It probably was the village's lame attempt to create some sort of modern business in a town that could not have changed much in a thousand years. Most likely, some local came into some money and somehow thought it was their chance to bring their town into the modern age. Whether they were right or wrong at this point did not make a difference, as all the inhabitants were surely either dead or infected.

The large white ceiling fan in the office lay still in the dark office. The room smelled of gunpowder and blood. The sun was just finishing its descent and Marty Rogers watched it with the reverence of one watching the last sunset of his life. He knew he should feel sad, maybe even angry. His life was most likely coming to an end. Worse even then that, his life may soon not belong to him any longer if he was to become one of the creatures that was now probably just outside their door. It seemed his destiny was now either to be consumed by a huge giant werewolf-like creature or to become one himself. The prospect of either was not a good one and he knew it. He knew his head should be screaming with it in fact. But there was a feeling that was overpowering everything. A feeling that kept fear from gripping his heart. Marty Rogers was hungry. In fact, he felt as if he was starving. He stared out at the sun knowing that the feeling was irrational and stupid but … it *was* nonetheless. He remembered the simple word scratched into Dr.

Edwards' journal. He knew what it meant but right now he didn't give a damn. Right now, he was nothing but plain hungry. He stared at the sunset not because of the beautiful colors and the serene setting as it descended below the sandy dunes of the desert. No, he concentrated on the sunset because the smell of the blood was almost too much for him to take. He knew damn well how disgusting his thoughts were right now, and that was the only reason he was not rushing over and gobbling handfuls of Siam into his mouth. He reached out miserably and plucked a dead beetle off the windowsill. He plopped it in his mouth and crunched it once before swallowing. Just the mere act of swallowing was blissful to him. He closed his eyes and enjoyed that very little amount of pleasure that the beetle gave him.

"Marty ... are you listening?" Jack asked him angrily, but Marty didn't care. In fact, he didn't care about anything anymore. That is, anything but finding something to eat. He heard the scrapes of claws on the mortar outside the window. Suddenly a feeling of jealous rage filled him as he thought of one of those creatures feeding on Siam's body when he was unable to. Why should that thing enjoy gorging itself when he had to stand here and suffer? No way was it going to enjoy that feeling when he had to resist! He heard the nails of the claws scraping just below where he could see. He stood on his toes looking down. He could just make out the tips of the thing's dark pointed ears.

"We have to do something!" Wendy was nearly hysterical. Jack paced the floor, rubbing his temples desperately as if willing a plan into his head. "COME ON JACK, we have to get out of here!" Wendy limped towards him, reaching out. She saw that Jack was watching something.

She looked over and watched as Marty moved quickly to the opposite wall. She thought he had such an angry look on his face that it looked close to madness. His eyes were wide, and his teeth were clenched in some sort of snarl. Marty leaned down and picked up the cabinet he had sent there as it was some kind of child's toy. A drawer opposite him fell out, filled with paper.

Jack jerked his head to the window, sensing movement. He noticed that the sky outside had suddenly become completely dark except for two yellow lights … no, not lights … eyes! The window burst apart and the darkness outside jumped in. It looked at them each with its ears nearly brushing the ceiling. Suddenly, there was a howl of rage but it didn't come from the creature.

Marty flung the cabinet at the monster. It hit with an incredible force, slamming against the windowsill and sending the creature behind it out the way it had come. They heard a satisfying thud as it hit the ground beyond.

"ALRIGHT!" Jack cheered, hands in the air.

"What do we do?" Wendy asked again, taking his arm. Jack went to the window and saw the creature getting off the ground and shaking its head, dazed. He noticed one of its clawed arms was hanging at an awkward angle. It looked up at him, snarling.

"Drag Siam over here," Jack said, walking to the window to look down.

"Why?" Marty asked seriously.

"We'll give 'em something to keep them busy."

"You mean just give him to them?" Marty asked back with shock and anger on his face.

"He's dead, Mart." Jack put his hands on Marty's shoulders. "I know it's a lot, but it just may buy us enough time to get out of here."

Marty looked down again at the creature as it hungrily and silently looked back at them. Marty wondered if it knew what they were planning and was just waiting patiently for its free meal. A meal it didn't deserve. He knew the pain of hunger and he kept in control. No way should he be able to go on feeling this way when it gets to eat. NO WAY!

"No." Marty said simply. "I won't let you."

"Dude, what's with the sudden concern with Elvis?" Jack asked, getting annoyed as time ticked by and their chances of escape got worse. Marty said nothing but crossed his arms and stared hard back at him.

Wendy slowly limped up next to Jack. "Marty…" She paused as if not wanting to say something. Jack looked at her curiously. "How about we go check for another way out and you … toss the body out the window … alone."

"No, I'm not gonna-" Marty paused and Jack looked at him confused. "Yes … okay." Marty's eyes lit up.

"What the f-" But before Jack could finish, Wendy dragged him to the other side of the room. "How'd you pull that off?" he asked her.

But then he heard something on the other side of the office door. It seemed there was slightly more light in the hall and he looked under the door at something moving. Jack put a finger to his lips and pulled his pistol. He stepped to the side of the door, aiming the gun where he thought whoever came through would be. He waved a hand to Marty to hold still, but Marty was already dragging the body of Siam to the window. He watched as Marty placed it on the windowsill; it seemed as if it became lodged on something. Marty's back was to him, and Jack watched Siam's legs bounce as Marty seemed to try to dislodge him. He heard a slight sniffle and looked behind him to see Wendy starting to cry. He put a hand up and made a soothing motion. He didn't dare speak and let whatever was outside hear him.

Suddenly, the door burst open and a soldier in desert fatigues stumbled several paces into the room. He recovered quickly and saw Jack and Wendy. Just as a word was about to escape his lips, a shadow flew into the room slamming the man flat to the ground. It was followed by another shadow and the man screamed as two dark forms ripped him apart on the floor in front of them. They watch, horrified, as the soldier looked up at the creatures, wide-eyed and terrified. Blood and flesh was flung everywhere. Just as Jack was about to turn away from the gruesome scene, the soldier's head came up to look at him. It was then covered by a black clawed appendage that slammed the head back onto the ground with a loud thud that sounded wet, and gore splashed around them. Jack turned his head and vomited on the wall.

"We should probably get going," Marty said, materializing next to them like some kind of ghost. "Come on, let's go." He calmly indicated the door as the two creatures frantically went about their business. Jack and Wendy followed him silently. He stopped and listened before leading them downstairs. The door to the building was open, letting in the last of the light. An empty desk, which was really a piece of wood on cinderblocks, sat to one side. It was obviously a crude attempt to create the persona of a receptionist. Probably something the rich villager had either seen on television or perhaps experienced in a real city somewhere.

Marty put an arm out and gently, but forcibly, pushed them into a wall beside the door instead of pushing them through. Just as their backs hit the wall, another one of the cursed creatures came into the building crouched close to the ground ... one of its appendages was curled up to its chest as it hung awkwardly. It stopped and rose to its full height. It put its long nose in the air and sniffed like a dog looking for the scent of the rabbit it was hunting. Problem was that they were the rabbit. Wendy closed her eyes and concentrated on not screaming. The creatures head snapped down when it caught the scent of what it was looking for.

Wendy didn't dare open her eyes, and when she suddenly felt someone pulling her, she nearly yelled.

"Hey," Jack said putting his hands on her face. "Mart said we should go now. Come on ... we got to keep moving." Wendy opened her eyes hoping that she would find herself back at the tent waking from a bad dream. "-got to go!" Jack insisted, taking her hand and pulling her towards the door. The pain that shot up her leg nearly made everything go dark. As she followed Jack out the door into the cool desert night in the abandoned village full of the cursed ones, she almost wished it had.

Jack looked around frantically but finally caught sight of Marty leaning against the well, smiling at them. He walked over with Wendy leaning her weight against him. As he approached, he noticed Marty's swollen belly.

"You suddenly get pregnant or something?" Jack asked him. But before Marty could answer, Wendy asked him which way.

"I have no idea," Marty shrugged. "I just came along for the beautiful beaches, man."

Jack laughed bitterly and looked around. They heard something coming down the dirt road and then saw the headlights of what looked like a jeep come towards them and moving fast. They ducked behind the well and waited for it to get closer. Jack peered over the stones and watched as the jeep went by. He ducked back down and rubbed his face like a man trying to contain himself.

"What?" Wendy asked.

"Dead guy slumped over the wheel."

Wendy leaned her head back against the rocks. Suddenly there was a crash and they jumped, looking at each other.

"The jeep," Jack said excitedly. "Maybe we can use it!" When he got no response, he looked over and saw Marty looking in the other direction where the jeep had come from.

"What now?" Jack asked, already feeling the hope run out of him.

"More jeeps coming," Marty said, still staring. "And..." He stopped, pausing. Jack watched him, thinking he could already picture him with pointed ears sticking up off his head as he concentrated on the sounds.

"-and what?" he asked, sure he didn't want the answer.

"-and more puppies ... maybe five or so."

"Ah, crap."

"Well, I'd rather be fishing," Marty said sarcastically, quoting the famous bumper sticker.

"Mart, can you tell how long before they get here?"

"My superpowers don't work like that."

Jack groaned, thinking. "Alright, I say we see if we can salvage the jeep that crashed."

Marty shook his head at him. "The puppies are there having their pre-dinner snack."

"So-" Wendy put in, still leaning back with her eyes closed. "It seems it's either throw ourselves on the mercy of Raul's little army or be Kibble and Bits. Sound about right?" Marty laughed at that like it was the funniest thing he had ever heard.

"We could wait for the showdown to go down here and try to disappear into the desert," Jack offered.

"And die tomorrow under the hot sun from dehydration," Wendy said, miserably. "-anybody carrying any water with them?"

"Nope," Marty said, smiling. He reached up and scratched his head. When he pulled back his hand, he found two of his dreadlocks still in his hand. "Thought I had until at least few years before that would happen." He looked up and saw Jack and Wendy staring at him. "Don't worry," he said, smiling at them. "I don't think Michelle was 'shtupping' me for my looks. I might look good bald!"

"Alright, we got to get Mart to a hospital," Jack said seriously. "New plan."

"Did we have one before?" Wendy asked.

"We go over to that jeep and use it to go to the hospital."

"Didn't we just go over that?"

Jack pulled his gun out and flipped off the safety.

"Cool!" Marty said excitedly. "So, we do the Butch Cassidy and Sundance Kid thing?"

"Didn't they die?" Wendy added.

"Not this time," Jack said standing up. "Enough. Let's do this."

"Hey, did anyone pick up Siam's gun?" Marty asked. Wendy rolled her eyes and pulled it from her bag. "Can I use it?" Marty asked like a child wanting to try out a new toy. Wendy looked over at Jack and he shrugged. Wendy sighed and handed it over. Marty bounced with enthusiasm.

"Somehow I don't think he's getting the gist of the situation," Jack said to Wendy. As he looked into Wendy's eyes, he immediately knew what she was thinking. She was thinking that Marty knew he was dead already and now he didn't give a damn. And that whatever was now inside him was changing him.

The plan was simple. Jack and Marty charged the jeep with guns blazing. They shot anything moving. Jack got in the jeep and tried to get it started while Wendy and Marty kept watch. The jeep started and they got the hell out of there. They all knew going into it that there were a lot of problems with the plan, but it was all they had. Marty was already showing signs of going through the change that they all now knew was coming. They had to get him to a hospital as soon as possible. And also, the small problem of Raul wanting to infect him and most likely shooting the other two in the head. And that's if they could make it alive with all the cursed monsters running around. The choices were limited. They chose their course and decided to go into it whole-heartedly. Jack only needed to take two deep breaths as he rested his hands on his knees.

Marty needed no convincing and bounced up and down excitedly and wanted to get moving. He still was feeling better than he had in a long time. Though he did know the craving was not far away. It was always there waiting to twist his mind and squeeze his stomach.

Wendy was no longer thinking at all. She had seen so many impossible things in one day. The implications of the Tomb of Arakis on

Egyptology. The meaning of finding werewolf-like creatures in the deserts of Egypt that seemed to come from some ancient-times disease. All of these things were far from her now. Right now, she only concentrated on one thing. That was putting weight on her leg and not having it buckle underneath her. The wound hurt so bad she just wanted to cry, but even as worn out as she was, she was not ready to give up. Not yet anyway.

"Shoot for the chest," Jack said, frowning as he stepped around the well and headed back towards the building. "Make 'em count, Mart."

It was very dark now. The only light was coming from the jeep headlights that were partially inside the building it had crashed into. It was too dark to tell how many were feeding off the dead man on the ground. They were just waves in the darkness. They came up close, unnoticed. Jack saw three of them and they were nearly finished with their meal. He could make out the bones of the dead soldier's ribcage even in the dim light. Jack pointed his gun and fired. The gunshot was loud, and Jack's ears rang from it. The three turned to look at him. The big gun had jerked up when he fired, and he had missed. Marty shot next. One of the cursed ones was thrown back by the impact of the bullet hitting its chest. Jack fired again, but the two remaining ones ran off into the darkness on all fours. The one Marty hit was still moving. Marty walked up and shot it twice more in the head. They were suddenly bathed in bright light. They shielded their eyes trying to see what it was. Then they heard Raul's voice telling them to drop their guns and step toward the jeep.

They looked at each other, not knowing what to do. Then there was shouting and gunfire beyond the light. They shielded their eyes trying to see but could only make out the light shifting back and forth and the sounds of the guns firing in rapid repetition. Then, as suddenly as it began, it ended. Everything was silent. But the light remained.

"What should we do?" Wendy whispered.

Jack tried so hard to see into the light that tears were running down his cheeks. "Ah ... hey," he tried. There was no reply. Jack detected movement and turned to Marty just in time to see him disappear out of the light. He called after him, but either Marty ignored him, or he couldn't answer. Seconds later, they heard the jeep start up. Then the light went off. When Jack and Wendy were able to see again, they saw Marty waving them towards the jeep as he sat in the driver seat, smiling.

"Where'd they go?" Jack asked as he ran towards him, but as if by answer they heard more gunshots in the darkness.

"I guess they tried to find someplace where they could better fight them off, Marty said, getting up and sliding into the backseat. "-don't think you guys want the terminally ill taking the wheel," he joked.

"First stop is the hospital, dude. Don't worry. We'll get through this." Jack got into the seat. When Wendy hopped awkwardly in with a groan of pain, Jack hit the gas.

"Any idea where we are?" Jack asked Wendy.

"They always kept the whereabouts hidden."

"So, you have no idea?"

"None."

"Great."

CHAPTER 20

IT CAME FROM THE SKY

Jack drove at moderate speed. Not because he was afraid of hitting anything or veering off the road. No, that was not what was making him keep nervously looking down at the dash. The problem was they had less then a quarter tank of gas. He was trying to keep the jeep at an even pace to conserve as much gas as possible. The constant focusing on the dash and then ahead of him was beginning to strain his eyes and his head was pounding.

Now that things were quiet, his guilt found an opportune time to surface. It gripped him like a vice. He was responsible for Marty. Everything and anything that happens to him here is because of him. He knew at this point that there was no use in *if* Marty was infected. The things he did back in the village were nothing like the old Marty. If he was to share the same fate as it seems his father had … then that would be on his head. He needed to get to a hospital quick. Jack looked in the rearview mirror and saw Marty looking around curiously. His swiveled a bit and Jack saw the glowing green reflection an animal has in their eyes when light bounces off them in the night. No, there was no *if*. His best friend in the world was on his way to becoming a cursed one, a monster, a fucking fictional creature from a million different stupid movies. How could this be happening?

He noticed Wendy looking behind them and worriedly glanced in the rearview mirror. Marty, too, was looking behind the jeep. He risked a look over his shoulder. He thought he saw lights, but he couldn't make out where exactly.

"Tell me Raul is right behind me," Jack said, his heart sinking.

"I think it's a plane," Wendy answered back.

"A plane?" Jack asked, confusedly. Then they heard the roar of the engines. "A plane!" he said more excitedly. "If it's landing, we can just follow the way it's going to a city!" As the roar of the engines came closer Jack started to get more excited. The first thing was to get Marty in a hospital. They had to have something that can help him. We still have a chance!

The plane went over their heads close enough for him to hit it with a rock.

"The runway must be close!" Jack yelled over the roaring engines. He hit the gas more enthusiastically to try to keep up. He chased it until they came to a cliff. They could have kept going to the right or watch where it landed and memorize the spot. Jack decided to stop the jeep and stood on his seat to watch. It looked just about ready to reach the ground. He saw it disappear out of sight behind a mound.

"Okay, that's it folks," he announced. "Everyone remember wh-" But before he could finish, the sky lit up from an explosion … exactly where the plane had 'landed.' They watched in silence as flames bounced in and out of view from the mound of desert sand that hid the actual site.

"You don't think-?" Wendy asked, stunned. Marty and Jack didn't say a word but remained staring with mouths wide.

"-no way," Wendy spoke out again. "It just can't be."

Jack let a burst of breath and rubbed his face. He slipped back down into the seat, his head now in his hands. He started laughing bitterly at the absurdity of it all.

"It's got to be something else. It just can't be." Wendy sat back down in her seat next to Jack. "I say we keep with the plan."

"You mean go and take in the horror show of an exploding jet?"

"No, I mean go see what really happened there. It's possible - I mean what are the odds that it exploded?"

"What else could it have been?" Jack asked, turning his head slightly towards her but still resting it on the steering wheel.

"Alright, let's say it was a crash. Well, that means things like firetrucks, anbulances, and whatever else come with a tragedy like that."

"The difference-" Marty interrupted. "-is instead of ambulances they have camels that just go-" Marty did his best impression of a sound of an ambulance coming from a camel's mouth.

"It's our best bet," Wendy said, ignoring him.

Jack silently nodded his agreement. "Okay … good thinking. Let's go." Wendy was surprised at how easily Jack had agreed. She had expected another debate. Then again, there really wasn't very much left to choose from.

"Instead of fire trucks-" Marty went on. "-they could just hike up their white dresses and piss it out." He stood in the back of the jeep and put his hands on himself as if he was taking a piss and made the sound of a fire siren.

"Those are not dresses ... asshole," Wendy said, holding on to the roll bar as the jeep bounced off the road towards the plane.

Jack could tell that they were getting closer. Every time they went up a hill the flames were visible and getting bigger. He was having a tough time finding areas where the jeep could go. Several times, he was sure that they would get stuck, but to the jeep's credit, it always pulled itself through whatever they put in front of it. Jack was sure, however, that his teeth would be significantly looser from the bouncy trip. But more than himself, he felt terrible about what it was doing to Wendy. Every time the jeep bounced, he was sure that she would scream out in pain and from the look on her face she was getting close to the breaking point. He was sure that if coming to the plane had been his own idea she would have already insisted that they stop. He had to admit he did admire the way she just gritted her teeth and took the punishment. She was nothing like the person he had thought she was. He decided in that moment that he really liked her. She was smart, strong, and able to hold her own with his smartass mouth.

"What is it?" she asked, seeing that he kept looking over at her.

"Nothing."

They bumped up again and she gave him a suspicious look.

Jack glanced in the mirror and saw Marty smiling back at him, wolfishly. Considering their situation, the look was more than a little disconcerting. He stopped the jeep suddenly and put on the brake.

Marty and Wendy looked at him, waiting for the reason he had stopped. He looked at Wendy and she shrugged a 'what the hell?' look at him.

"We don't know what we're going to find over that hill," Jack said seriously. "I just want everyone to be prepared."

"I'm good," Marty said cheerfully. Too cheerfully for Jack's liking.

"After today, what can shock me?" Wendy put in.

"Alright," Jack simply said and put the jeep back in first gear.

They went up the hill and, once again, Jack stopped the jeep. They all stared at what lay before them. Jack thought to himself that he could take the *if* out of this scenario as well. The jet lay on its side on top of a broken wing. The other wing was broken off several feet away. Flames burned in pockets all around it. Most of it was black and charred. All over the sand around the plane were small bundles of whatever had been inside it. They knew that at least some of these were the remains of the people. Seeing the mangled twisted metal, they suspected that there would be no survivors. One of the fires burst upwards as it found something else to burn.

"I saw this bird on the Discovery Channel, you know," Marty said, staring at the carnage. "It would fly into an already occupied nest when the mother was gone looking for food. It would just sit and wait for the bird to fly out of the nest, you know, look for food or something, and then it would swoop in."

"I don't want to hear about bad birds eating other's eggs," Wendy said miserably.

"Not where I was going, Miss Pessimism. What I was going to tell you is that this bird would lay its egg right there in that nest next to the others. She would lay her egg and just … leave. Who knows, maybe she went to Boca Raton or West Palm Beach but all I'm saying is she laid that egg and left."

"So?" Jack asked, scratching his chin blankly.

"So … the other bird came back and was none the wiser. She raised that other bird as her own, never realizing the difference."

"I don't get the point," Wendy said.

"Okay, guys. Here we go, so try to get all the neuro-transmitters you have left working. *We* are the egg … get it."

Jack paused to think before answering. "What the hell are you talking about?" he finally asked, exasperated.

"I think I get it," Wendy said at last. "You're saying we become the survivors of this plane crash?"

"You got it." Marty smiled.

"Why?"

"Think about it," Marty smiled. "Here we are in Egypt, somewhere, with no passports or anything; I know mine is back there." He jabbed a thumb the way they had come. "We tell any of them the story of what happened to us, and we'll be here forever."

"But if we're part of this crash," Wendy smiled, "we get swept up and taken directly to the hospital. Not to mention lots and lots of people who would notice Raul trying to take us away. You get it?"

"What do we tell the Egyptians when they ask why there are three Americans on the plane?" Jack asked skeptically.

"Interns," Marty said, making a 'kissy' face at him.

"The rest we could make up as we go," Wendy added, giving Marty a dark look.

"Alright then," Jack said, shrugging his agreement with the plan. "You guys go down there and get comfortable. I'll go ditch the jeep. You sure people are coming?" He asked Wendy.

"They're coming."

CHAPTER 21
THE HOSPITAL

Wendy was right. In under an hour, a helicopter circled the site. Fifteen minutes after that, three more showed up and landed. Men in military uniforms wearing red bands around their arms searched the area for survivors. When they were located, they were bundled into stretchers, put into the helicopters, and given first aid. Wendy's pants were cut off and her leg was bandaged. All three were given IV's. Jack felt a hand go into his pocket and knew they were searching for identification. He wished he had had the hindsight to hide his wallet. He heard several men speaking in Egyptian as they looked at it. Then he heard his name being given into a walkie-talkie. He only dared open his eyes slightly, so as not to give away their ruse. Suddenly he heard a commotion near the still-burning plane. He let his head flop over as if he was in pain but really trying to get a better look through the door. He saw two men running towards the plane with another stretcher in their hands. He was surprised to see the men so anxious to remove a dead body. He saw another man following just as quickly with a first aid kit. Then the helicopter door slammed shut and he heard the propeller start increasing speed. Next thing he knew he started to feel warm and sleepy. He realized they must have given him a drug for his perceived pain. Then there was only darkness.

Wendy kept hearing an insistent beeping that wouldn't stop pulling her from her sleep. She was dreaming that she had married Ralph Lumbard from her freshman micro-economics class. He was a quiet boy with long bangs that hid his large brown eyes. Whenever Wendy would catch the boy looking at her from across the classroom, his eyes would get as big as saucers, and he would look away. She remembered on one occasion when, out of curiousity, she dropped her pencil by his desk to see if he would talk to her. She even hesitated a moment before walking away. She had glanced over at him to see him staring intently at the professor as if she didn't even exist. She remembered being so mad she could have slapped him on his big head. But that was when he turned shyly to her and gave her a half smile. She knew in that smile that he could be hers if she wanted him.

That was the same day she had met with the perverted calculus professor. She wondered how different her life would have been if it had not been for that bastard. Perhaps she and Ralph would be married and living in suburbia bliss somewhere in upstate Connecticut with their three kids and a golden Labrador retriever named Max.

Wendy sighed in her sleep, feeling the beeping once again pulling her from her dreams. She tried to imagine what it would be like to have to drive a minivan full of screaming kids. She thought it would be heaven compared to the damn incessant beeping. *What the hell is that!* She opened eyes with clenched teeth and followed the sound with her eyes to the monitor that she knew, at once, was following her heart rate. *Oh, yeah.* She thought miserably. *Awaken from the dream to the nightmare.*

"Ah! You have decided to join us, I see," a woman said from somewhere beside her. She looked around groggily and finally saw a woman in a doctor's coat standing by her feet looking at a chart.

199

"Where am I?" Wendy asked, a little surprised at just how weak her voice sounded.

"You are at the Cairo Hospital," the doctor said, putting down the chart and coming to stand beside her. "You are a remarkable woman," the doctor said, shaking her head at her. "There is no explanation as to why you should be alive."

Wendy noticed the suspicious way the doctor tilted her head. It was as if to say 'No way you were on that plane. What are you up to?'

"Just lucky, I guess?" Wendy smiled, trying to seem just as baffled.

"Still..." The doctor paused, smiling tightly. "Not as lucky as your friends."

"Are they alright?" Wendy sat up and felt a distant pain her thigh. She winced and the doctor looked at her leg. "That is healing very nicely," the doctor said.

"My friends-" Wendy looked around the small room for the first time. She noticed the bars on the windows.

"If another day went by it would have been impossible to stitch. You have to get at it within at least the first couple days."

"Could you please tell me about my friends?" *Did she say a couple of days? How long have I been out?*

The white curtain blocking what she suspected was the door was flung to the side and a man in desert fatigues faced her with an angry look. He held an M16 machine gun across his shoulder easily like he had been born with it.

"Who are you?" he asked in his deep accent.

"My friends?" Wendy answered back defensively. The man stepped forward, but the doctor stepped in front of him talking in Egyptian in soothing tones. The man finally stepped back and left the room.

"You must not coax them," the doctor said, now sounding more like a mother then a doctor. "They are very dangerous men and you and your friends, who are fine, should take care dealing with them."

Wendy sank back into the bed and sighed. She wondered what kind of mess she was in now. She looked up at the ceiling and decided that no matter how bad it was it couldn't be any worst than being with the cursed. Just as the thought left her head, a scream that became a howl filled her room.

"Oh, my God!" Wendy pulled the sheet from the bed and attempted to jump off.

"Whoa!" The doctor shouted, putting her hands on her shoulders. "That's just another survivor from the plane. Nothing that will hurt you."

Wendy looked into the woman's eyes and saw that she actually believed it.

Stupid woman! That is exactly what will hurt us all!

Jack stopped pacing his room as the howl cut through the silence. *Please don't let that be Marty ... please God, not Marty.* He suddenly had a frantic urge to get out of the room. He knew the bars were on the window, but maybe he could pull one of them loose and squeeze through. He could get out, find Wendy and Marty, and get the hell away from this place. He grabbed one of the bars and tried to shake it loose. He pulled with everything he had, but it didn't even budge. He put one foot on the wall, closed his eyes, and strained until he thought his head would explode.

"You have somewhere you need to be?"

Jack jumped to attention, looking around the room for the person who had spoken. He found the soldier sitting comfortably in the chair next to the bed. Jack wondered how long he had been there.

"You seem ... agitated," the man said, pulling a cigarette out of his pocket and lighting it. "Aren't you worried about the other survivor making all that noise? It almost seems like you were trying to get away from whoever that poor bastard might be?" The soldier blew out a large cloud of smoke and stared at him through it with dark cruel eyes. "Why do you suppose that would be?"

"I..."

"You know, I have my theory. Would you like to hear it?" The man went on, not waiting for an answer. "I think you are some American spy that was sent to kill whoever was on that plane. That's what I think.

You know what we do to spies in my country?" The man smiled, showing off his brown-stained teeth.

"I'm not a spy," Jack said angrily.

"No?" The man stood from the chair and Jack realized what a big man he was. "Let's say we just find that out."

Jack saw the rifle leaning on the wall behind him. The soldier followed his gaze and turned to look at the gun as well. "Tell you what, spy," he said, turning back and smiling again. "If you can get to it, you can have it."

"Listen to me," Jack put up his hands and started backing up. "I'm no spy. I'm just a college kid, man! Please…"

"Please? That is the smartest thing you said so far. No more games." The man reached into his pocket and brought out a pair of black gloves. "We're gonna have some fun."

"You're making a mistake!" Jack said looking around desperately. "I'll tell you anything you want to know. Anything!"

"Yes, boy. You will." The soldier took two quick steps forward and started pounding as Jack tried to cover his head as the blows just kept coming. He came to realize the gloves must have some kind of metal in them and his head, back, and arms screamed with pain as the man unmercifully rained pain down on him. Jack fell to the ground in a fetal position and at once realized his mistake. The man started kicking at him with his big black boots. Jack yelled for him to stop at first, but soon the pain and effort of yelling was too much. The light started to fade, and he was thankful.

"Oh, no you don't, American!" The man picked him up and slammed him against the wall. "You fall asleep, and you wake up missing something." The man reached between Jack's legs and squeezed.

"NO!" Jack screamed as a new kind of pain burst into his head. The man let go and Jack opened his eyes immediately, knowing the punishment that would come if the soldier thought he passed out. He stared at the back of the man's head, confused. He looked down and saw the man's hands still holding him up on the wall. It didn't make sense. He shook his head trying to clear it, afraid he might already be passing out again. Fear ran up his spine as he thought the soldier could already be hacking off his manhood. Suddenly the grip loosened, and the big soldier fell to the floor. Jack's legs felt weak, but he stayed up. He slowly looked up to see Marty standing close to where the soldier had just been. Marty was smiling as if he had just heard a new joke.

"That guy was sick, dude," Marty said, scratching absently at a large patch of black skin on his face.

Jack felt the world tilt and then knew he was falling.

Next thing he knew, the soldier was once again facing him smiling his rotten mouth grin. "I told you what I would do, boy." Jack felt him grab him and the soldier leaned his head back and howled like one of the cursed ones. When his head snapped back, he had the head of a canine with yellow eyes bright with rage.

Jack opened his eyes and yelled, grabbing his groin. "NO!" he yelled.

"Jack, it's alright." It was Wendy's voice as he looked around the room still holding his groin.

"I'm right here," Wendy said, putting a hand on his shoulder. "You are safe."

Another howl filled the room.

"What happened?"

"You passed out," Wendy said, sitting down on the bed that Jack was in. "Marty um … arrived and brought you here."

Jack followed her eyes to the wall, and he looked to see a big hole. Pieces of sheetrock hung in pieces around it. "He saved me."

"Yes, Jack." Wendy nodded. "Marty brought you here with us."

"Where is he?"

"He is … in the other room."

Jack started to get off the bed, but Wendy gently pushed him back. "I think you should leave him alone."

"What-why?"

Wendy sighed. Jack thought she looked very sad. "He is almost gone, Jack."

"Gone? Gone where?"

"I think you know."

"Oh, no." Jack shook his head. "No ... no ... NO!" He got off the bed, pushing Wendy's hand aside. He ran to the hole in the wall and peered inside. He saw Marty's back and tried to make out what he was doing. He almost called out when he realized what was going on. He saw the body of the soldier moving side to side as Marty pulled him apart. Jack realized his best friend in the world was eating a dead man. The realization made the blood in his veins go cold. Suddenly Marty froze and put his nose in the air. Jack watched, not able to move.

"You should leave," Marty said, without turning.

"Mart, I am so sorry." Marty started laughing bitterly, but not turning.

"Dude ... there still might be a way-" Jack tried.

"To save me?" Marty asked, turning to Jack now. Jack sucked in a breath and stepped back. Marty's face was almost entirely black with one piercing yellow eye. One of his ears was poking out from the side of his head. It was pointed and seemed to be on its way to the top of his head. "You think that after doing this-" Marty indicated the dead soldier with a nod of his head. "-that I could go on being Marty the friendly pothead?"

"We could-"

"Forget it!" Marty snarled. "Game over, dude. My future is preordained. I know what's going to happen and to tell you the truth-" Marty paused to smile and show off his blood-stained sharp-looking fangs. "It feels pretty good."

Jack saw tears start to roll down his friend's face.

"Jack, just do me one favor."

"Anything buddy."

Marty paused wiping the tears from his face. "Kill me."

"Oh, Mart." Jack felt his own tears coming now.

"You owe me," Marty said, putting his head in his now claw-like hands. "Just do it ... JUST DO IT!"

"I just-"

"Here." Jack saw a gun come sliding towards him to where he stood in the hole in the wall. Just as it hit the wood by his feet, the door to the room Marty was in exploded apart. In the doorway stood a cursed one that looked as if should have been dead long ago. It had almost no fur left on its body. Even the skin hung in patches around it. One of its ears looked to be melted to the side of its head. It held a clawed arm to its chest and it also looked as if that, too, had been melted into its body. It dragged a canine leg as it limped into the room. Jack watched it focus on the bloody half-eaten corpse. Saw as its one remaining eye opened wide with excitement.

Marty also saw what it wanted and stood snarling viciously at it.

Jack snatched up the gun and pointed at the monster. Just as he was about to fire, Marty moved across the room faster then Jack would have ever thought possible and slammed into it. They disappeared from his view. He could hear them fighting like wild dogs just outside.

Jack felt a hand on his shoulder and jumped, raising the gun up. "WAIT!" Wendy said holding up her hands.

"Jesus! What are you doing?" Jack swore at her.

"We should go … when we still can."

"And leave him?"

"He is already gone, Jack," Wendy said, putting her hands on her hips. "If we're going to get out of this alive, we need to go!" She grabbed his shirt and pulled him towards the door.

He saw a woman standing off to the side in what looked to be a white doctor's jacket. She watched them in what looked like shock. "Who's she?" Jack asked.

"She's a doctor." Wendy shrugged. "She's been like that since Marty came through the wall."

"Should we take her with us?" The doctor slowly started shaking her head.

Wendy watched her. "Guess she wants to take her chances here."

"Fine," Jack said, heading for the door. "I can't believe we're just going to leave him." He reached for the door and turned the knob. "Shit!" The door was locked. "We gotta find another way out." He looked again at the woman. "Does she have keys?"

"She would knock and they let her out," Wendy said, frowning.

"Who?" Jack asked confused.

"The soldiers outside the door."

"So where are they now?"

"I think that thing outside scared them off."

"Some soldiers," Jack said bitterly, looking through the hole Marty had made to the other room. "He tried not to look at the half-eaten body that still lay there. He heard Marty and that thing still fighting, but it seemed he thought they were further away. He wondered if there was enough of Marty left that he was fighting on purpose so they could escape. He wanted to think there wasn't, as it made the decision to leave him just a bit easier. "Let's go." He grabbed Wendy's hand, stepped through the hole, and headed for the door.

He peeked outside the door and looked up and down the hall. There was not a soul around and the fighting seemed ever further away now. He thought it was strange that there would be no one in a hospital. They were supposed to be in the Cairo Hospital … how could there be no one? The hall to the left seemed to go on forever as the overhead ultraviolet lights led the way. It was an easy decision as the fighting was somewhere to the right. They ran down the hall, looking into the rooms but seeing nobody in them. They recognized a sign with an elevator and headed for it. They made two turns following the sign and finally they found it. Jack pushed the buttons frantically as they both kept looking back; they had been expecting the cursed one to be there looking back at them. They watched the lights to the elevator go on twice, but the doors never opened.

"It's not stopping," Jack said at last, hearing the elevator only inches from them behind the wall passing them again.

"Why would they do that?"

"If you heard that thing, would you want to stop on this floor?"

Wendy dropped her head in her hands and started to cry.

"Are you alright?" Jack asked, putting his hands on her shoulders, unsure if he should. To his surprise, Wendy stepped forward and buried her head in his chest. It still hurt from the soldier's beating but somehow it didn't make a difference. He wrapped his arms around her and squeezed. They clung together as they listened to the elevator passing them up and down.

"We'll get out of here," Jack said, unsure he believed it. Wendy did not respond but she did stop crying. "I think maybe if we find the stairs." Wendy still did not respond. "Hey, I think we should probably keep moving." Wendy pulled away, sniffling. "I think we should keep moving," he tried again.

Wendy looked up and saw what looked to be a closet opposite them. She looked down at her hospital gown, frowning. She saw that somehow Jack still had his clothes. She thought that strange and somehow that made her angry. She walked to the closet and turned the handle. It was unlocked. Jack followed her inside, closing the door, unsure what she was doing. Wendy searched the room, finding what she was looking for on a top shelf. It was doctor scrubs. She took off her gown and ripped at the plastic containing the scrubs. She stopped halfway, putting the pants on. She noticed her wound looked much better. In fact, it felt better too. At least one thing to be thankful for, she thought bitterly. She felt Jack's eyes on her. She looked over thinking he too was looking at her wound. As she looked, she noticed her wound was the only thing he wasn't looking at. She pulled on the pants and shirt quickly.

"I will never understand men," she said, tying her hair back with some twine she found. "How does anything ever get done when your minds are always on one thing ... all the freak'n time?"

Jack just smiled, shrugging. Then they heard a snort from under the door. They looked at each other, wide-eyed, and Jack cursed silently. Wendy looked around the room frantically. She saw in the back of the room a silver-like door built into the wall. She nodded towards it and Jack looked. He mouthed the question 'what?' Wendy knew they had no time for conversation and moved towards it on her tiptoes. They heard another sharp intake of breath as she moved. Instead of freezing, however, she picked up her pace.

Jack didn't know what to do. He looked back at the door and saw the handle slowly turn. The door swung open and, in the doorway, was the dark shape of a cursed one. It slowly came inside, staring into his eyes. Jack recognized it as the burned one Marty was just fighting with. He thought it somehow now looked better already. It was still covered in burns but now there were tuffs of black fur in some places. As Jack's eyes ran up the muscular body, he saw the arm was still melted to its chest. However, the ear that he thought was totally burned off seemed to be growing back. Even in his terror he thought it amazing. The cursed one stepped forward, spreading its arm. The other moved eerily around its chest. The creature looked down at it angrily. He watched the muscles of the creature flex and then it caught its breath. He watched as the melted arm slowly pulled away from the flesh of the torso. Jack thought it sounded not unlike sheets ripping. Blood ran down its legs onto the floor. The cursed one still held its breath and caught Jack's eye as it pulled. Jack saw no sign of pain … only rage. When the arm came all the way free, hanging with dead flesh and blood, it howled with both arms raised with what sounded like victory. Its head snapped back down to meet Jack's eyes. It snarled, showing off already blood-soaked teeth. Jack thought about the doctor and wondered if that blood was hers. Then a shelf came down, flattening the beast to the ground.

"You coming or what!" Wendy said frantically. Jack shook his head and looked at her. His eyes stung from not blinking. "Dumb-ass … come on!"

Jack woke from his spell and ran towards her, still shaking his head and trying to clear it. She grabbed his hand and pulled him towards the metal door in the wall.

"What's that?" he asked.

"Not sure."

"You're not thinking of..." But before he could finish, she already had the door open and was pulling him into it with her. As Jack was diving in, he saw it was some kind of metal chute. He hoped it was for the linens and not for things like needles and bio waste. Then he was falling. He thought he passed light twice but was moving too fast to really tell. One time he even thought he saw someone but couldn't be sure. Whoever it was, he was sure they had a huge nose.

No ... Raul!

Then they landed on something soft, but the impact still knocked the wind out him. Then the pain came as he realized he had fallen onto Wendy's knee in the very worst spot. He curled up in a fetal position trying to catch his breath.

"Why does it ... always have to be like this?" he asked, holding himself.

"You would think as much as you love that thing you would take better care of it," Wendy said, getting up awkwardly in the pile of hospital laundry. Then they heard the rumbling of something else coming down the chute ... something big. Suddenly the pain between his legs was gone.

213

It was coming fast. Wendy got up and kicked the wall beside them hard. Suddenly they were moving. Jack realized that they were in a laundry cart. They rolled away from the chute and together, they turned around, trying to see what was coming. At first, he thought it was more laundry as something wrapped in cloth hit the cement. If it were not for the huff of breath as it hit he would not have known it was a man. Jack saw his rifle slide across the floor as it landed, following him.

"Get it!" Wendy yelled to him. Jack jumped up, nearly falling on his face, and snatched up the gun. Just as he did, something else came down the chute. The man who hit the ground slowly rolled onto his back and looked up. Seconds later, he was screaming as he stared up. The cursed one hit him with a horrible crunch.

Jack and Wendy turned and ran, looking for a way out. Sheets were hanging everywhere. As they ran, they brushed them aside. Jack thought they would never end. It was dark and there was steam so he couldn't see the ground and, just as he thought it was a matter of time before he tripped, he felt something wrap around his foot. He fell, taking Wendy with him. He saw something fly over him. He looked up, seeing the cursed one sliding on its belly away from him in the steam. He saw its single yellow eye as it disappeared into the darkness.

Wendy was the first to spring up and pull him to his feet. They ran towards the light. They tossed the hanging sheets away from them, finding a door. Someone was standing there. It was a short man with sheets in his arms. He stared at them as they ran past. Then there was a howl. They saw the man turn towards them as they ran. The hall was bright, and they shielded their eyes.

"An elevator!" Jack said grabbing Wendy's hand.

When they got there, Jack hit the button and the elevator 'dinged' as it opened. Jack smiled to Wendy. Just then the man who had been holding the sheets slammed into a wall and the cursed one came around the corner on all fours, snarling wildly.

"Get in!" Jack pushed Wendy inside and glanced back as he stepped in. He saw the cursed one start to run towards them on all fours. Jack hit the button to close the elevator.

"Come on! Come on!" he yelled as the doors took an eternity to shut. They heard something hit the closed doors and they stepped back.

"Hit a button!" Wendy whispered frantically. Jack reached looking at the buttons confused. "Which one?"

"Who cares!"

Jack reached out and picked the number four. The elevator started moving and they breathed. A song played a Musak version of 'Walking on Sunshine' from Katrina and the Waves. They looked at each other but they were too tired and scared to see the humor in it. Just then the doors opened and they moved back from them, wide-eyed and not sure what was going to be there. An Egyptian family moved inside, looking at them suspiciously. They were a middle-aged couple with what seemed to be their young daughter and aging father. The doors shut and they breathed easier as they started moving again.

"Why didn't you hit one?" Wendy asked.

"What?"

"Number one," Wendy said again. "If that's the main floor we could get out of here."

"Are you kidding me?"

"No, we could be heading for the door right now."

Jack coughed in disbelief. "How do you know we were not already on one? What if I hit that number and the doors opened again? Are you nuts?" He noticed it became quiet again, other than the annoying music, and looked around at the family staring at him. Then something hit the elevator. It rocked sideways slightly, and a woman screamed. Jack looked up nervously. He heard scraping sounds but couldn't tell where it was coming from. He looked over at Wendy and saw her staring wide-eyed at the floor. He followed her gaze and saw a part of the floor bending open.

"Oh, come on!" he said, watching the floor in one corner opening up. The elder man walked over to investigate. He poked the floor with his foot as if testing it. Jack was about to pull him back when a black clawed arm shot through the hole and grabbed him. The man was slammed to the ground. The family grabbed for his arms as the man screamed. He was pulled towards the small hole. His leg disappeared

216

and then there was a crunch. The man stopped screaming and the family was able to pull him away from the hole. He came away easily from the hole and they noticed his leg was missing. Blood started squirting everywhere from the stub. They all stood staring in shocked silence as they became covered with it. Then the doors opened. Jack and Wendy were first to exit. They looked back to see the elevator doors closing again with the entire family looking at them wide-eyed but not saying a word. A second later, the doors were being forced open again by claws.

"Run!" Jack said, taking Wendy's hand again. They ran down the hall with people staring at them. They took a corner and ran past a waiting room. They both looked in as they ran and saw Raul and a handful of soldiers watching them as they ran past.

"Things just got worse!" Wendy said as they ran. They heard Raul shouting after them and then there was gunshots and screaming. They knew that the cursed one in the elevator had caught up with the soldiers. They pushed through double doors that led to what looked like an ICU. Wendy's breath burned in her throat, and she pulled Jack into one of the rooms. She shut the door and pulled the curtain around to block its view.

"We-" Jack stopped taking a breath. "We can't stop here."

Wendy nodded, putting her hands on her knees and breathing.

"I can't believe-" Jack took a breath. "-our friend Raul is here."

"He's probably here to finish the job." Wendy answered miserably.

He's gotta catch us first," Jack said, trying to sound brave. For the first time since entering the room, he noticed a strange flashing of light in the room. He looked around and saw that it was coming from the window.

"Sirens?" Wendy asked, seeing what he was up to.

"Doesn't seem like it." He walked to the window and looked down. At first it was hard to see between the smoke. He started to make out the parameter of soldiers and military vehicles. He realized the hospital must be surrounded by them. In between the hospital and the soldiers and vehicles there was smoke. Every now and again there was a flash of light. Long bursts of light. He concentrated on trying to see. Wendy came beside him, and they both squinted, staring down with their heads pressed against the window. There was a sudden breeze and the smoke shifted. They saw a woman running towards the soldiers with her hands above her head. She was wearing a patient's gown and still had wires from the IV hanging from her arm. There were two flashes of light and the woman stopped and fell over face first onto the ground. Jack and Wendy's mouths fell open as realization came to them. They watched as men in hazsuits walked towards the woman. They carried what looked to be cylinders on their backs.

"Oh, my god," Wendy whispered, watching them.

"What's he going to do?" As if by answer, the man in the suit stood beside the woman and raised what Jack thought was a gun. Even through the smoke they could see the woman raising an arm slowly from the ground.

"She's still alive!" Jack said, pressing his head more firmly against the window.

There was a spark and then lines of fire shot from the man. The woman was engulfed immediately. The man relentlessly kept his flame on her. When he stopped, all that was left was a charred corpse with an outstretched arm. There were more shots in the smoke and the man in the suit disappeared into the smoke again. Jack and Wendy looked towards the charred woman again and saw the arm break in half, falling to the ground.

"They're killing everyone in this hospital," Wendy said, as if it made perfect sense. Jack pulled away from the window and looked at her. "Don't you see?" she asked, her blue eyes wide now and tears threatening to roll down her cheeks. "It's the only way to be sure it doesn't get out." Her voice started to get frantic. "They have to kill us all!" She walked over to Jack and grabbed his shoulders in a tight grip. "We cannot leave here alive, Jack." Jack could see the pain and weariness in her eyes. "If we are infected there is no telling what would happen to all the people outside." Wendy lowered her head and pressed it into his chest again. "Don't you see … we can't survive."

Jack gently put a hand under chin and lifted her head. Wendy's eyes were closed when he looked down at her face. He watched as her eyes fluttered like they wanted to open but something was keeping them closed. Jack leaned down slightly and pressed his lips against hers. To his surprise, she pressed back into him. In fact, she straightened and leaned against him. She was not wearing a bra and her breasts felt warm

219

and soft pressed on him. Jack put his hands on her back and pressed her firmly to him as they kissed deeply. When she pulled away, Jack left his eyes closed a few seconds, savoring the moment. He had no idea he had these types of feelings for Wendy. His head swam with it.

"Jack?" Wendy said softly.

"Yeah, I was just-" he froze, trying to understand what was in front of him. Near the bed by the window, Wendy stood nude in the flashing of light. He watched as she reached up and shook her blond hair loose from its binding. As she did, the flashing from the window gave him quick glances of her toned body. He knew it was morbid wishing for more flashes of light to see her when each one meant someone outside the window was dying below them. He stepped towards her thinking of nothing else but her. Wendy reached out her arms and stepped towards the bed. Jack moved fast and had her again in his arms. He kissed her neck, thinking how good her skin smelled and tasted. He ran his hands down her backside. Wendy spun around and pressed her back into him. Jack let his hands explore her and Wendy moaned. She grabbed his hand and pulled him roughly to the bed.

They did not know how much time had passed. The light outside would stop awhile and then start up again as if it never ended. They knew there must be people still trapped in the building. What a predicament to be in. Either wait it out in the hospital with the cursed ones or run for safety outside only to get shot and probably burned alive. Either way, it left them dead.

220

Jack and Wendy watched through the hospital window, still nude and wrapped in each other arms. They held on to each other like the whole world had been plunged into water and they were the only thing that still floated. Wendy curled into him, and Jack held her tight in his arms. She stroked his forearms as they watched through the window.

"You must be dehydrated," Wendy said in a gentle voice. Jack just chuckled and brushed her hair out of her face. "You have any ideas?"

Jack thought before answering. His head was swimming about Wendy, so it was hard to get a solid thought. But on the other side of that, with her in his arms, for some reason he was feeling like he could do anything. Wendy rolled back slightly to look at him.

"You keep moving like that and thinking is going to be impossible," he said. Wendy smiled at him and turned to face him. She pushed him back towards the bed. She kissed his mouth and sat on top of him. Jack did not need any persuasion. Wendy leaned forward on top of him, putting her hands on the bars on the side of the bed. Jack let his head roll backwards and suddenly the room was filled with the sounds of sirens and flashing lights. Jack looked around, alarmed, and Wendy jumped off of him to lie beside him. Jack saw the television and found the control on the arm of the bed. He grabbed it and lowered the volume. They both were hypnotized by what was going on there. There was a woman reporter with long straight black hair, long nose, and thick red lipstick speaking in Egyptian and pointing to pictures of soldiers as they fired their weapons at a building. It did not take long to realize that those soldiers were firing at their building. The Cairo General Hospital. Jack thought it strange hearing the gunshots come over the television several seconds after they went off outside.

"What are they saying?" Jack asked. Wendy held up a finger for him to wait. After a few more seconds, Wendy turned to him with a bitter smile on her face. "What is it?"

"Terrorists."

"What! You gotta be kidding me!"

"Nope." Wendy shook her head. "It seems the hospital has been taken over by Al Quida and that they are holding the people inside prisoner."

"So how do they explain shooting the people outside?" Jack asked, stepping out of the bed and walking to the window.

"They are saying that the many Al Qaeda inside have tried to escape into the city. They are saying the military is keeping the city safe. They are getting one thing right."

"What's that?"

"They are saying the terrorists may have some biological weapon inside. I guess that's accurate … in a way."

"I would say it is very accurate," Raul answered, spinning the curtain around the pole. He saw them naked and turned away as if he were about to get sick. Jack and Wendy exchanged a confused look.

"Will you animals put your clothes on, please?" He ended the plea with some words in what Jack assumed was Egyptian. He looked over to see if Wendy understood it and could see by the light of the television that her face was very red. "What did he say?" Jack asked, looking for his pants on the floor. "It seems our friend Raul here hates us with every fiber of his soul," Wendy whispered, finding her clothes on the floor.

"I guess in his religion their souls are made up of *fiber*," Jack said, imitating a professor back home. "You see, that would be the only logical explanation for all the shit they keep flinging at us." Wendy snorted a quick laugh.

"ENOUGH!" Raul roared. "You two have caused quite enough trouble, I think." He leaned outside the curtain, giving orders before turning back. "So, son of a thief. Did you enjoy your little father-son reunion?"

"What are you talking about?" Jack asked, sliding on his doctor shoes that he got from the closet before jumping through the laundry chute. "And who are *you* to be insulting my father, Raul?"

"Who am I?" Raul shouted. "I am of the last of the warriors that fight to see that Egypt does not become a western toy to play with. To see that you and your kind do not rape our people and lands to the point where there is nothing left of mother Egypt." He stopped to spit on the ground. "You and your kind make me sick. You come here to pull our bones and history from the earth to make yourself rich. Meanwhile that which has made us gets traded in dark alleys or by rich men who would

223

just as soon use the burial mask of Great Ramses as an ash tray. You people come here and take and take with no concern for what you are doing to my country. Meanwhile, we get your western cancers. You bring your McDonalds and your pizza, and your western customs and my people suffer as they try to be like you. Like you!" Raul coughed up something and spat on the floor again. "Ah, let us speak about the good doctor Edwards, shall we?"

Wendy and Jack exchanged a nervous look.

"Your father is everything we hate about you."

"Who's we?" Jack asked.

Raul paused, staring at him angrily as trying to decide if he should tell them. "I am a warrior of Thoth. My people are here to protect Egypt from ones like you."

"I thought Thoth was the god of knowledge ... a god that kept the scriptures of what goes on in Egypt."

"My god-" Raul started looking at Wendy dangerously, "Would be the one to protect the things that are being stolen everyday. It would be Thoth in his infinite wisdom that would see by stealing our history, our scriptures, and even our bones that you are taking away all things that have made us Egyptians. You are bleeding the soul of Egypt and now you all will pay." A howl filled the halls outside. Raul smiled. "Daddy's home."

"So, wait," Wendy said stepping forward. "So, if I get this right, you and your buddies of Thoth-"

"Watch it." Raul warned, waving a finger dangerously.

"Alright … sorry. So, you and the other warriors came across the Anubis scroll."

"We found it hidden in an ancient sarcophagus that was stolen from us."

"You robbed a museum?" Jack asked, shaking his head. "And I bet you just returned it to the ground, right?" Raul said nothing. "Or, perhaps you, too, sold the sarcaphogus … maybe as a Thoth fundraiser or something? Perhaps washing cars in bikinis was beneath you?"

Raul put his hand on his gun and unclipped the cover. Wendy gave Jack a dirty look and went on trying to win back his attention.

"So, the scroll, Raul. What did it say?"

"It told of an ancient Priest who tried to use the power of the curse to rid Egypt of its enemies. It told of such a powerful curse that it could lay waste to whole kingdoms. It told of Anubis and his magic and darkness for those that attack mother Egypt. It is no mistake that it is Anubis that weighs the heart in death. He is a powerful ally to Thoth and his curse will rid us of your Western ways. In fact, we had a plan to be rid of the West all together." Raul frowned viciously.

"My god, Raul," Jack said, thinking he knew what he was up to. "You mean for us to bring this plague back to the U.S. and wipe out millions?"

"Yes." Raul shrugged. "Of course."

"How do you keep the whole world from being infected … even here," Wendy asked, shaking her head. "This could sweep the globe, Raul … or whoever you are. You'd be killing yourself."

"Our god will keep us safe." Raul smiled confidently. "This will be the death of the evil of your home."

"Where did you find it?" Jack asked, shaking his head. "How could this thing exist thousands of years later."

Raul smiled and crossed his arms proudly. "The virus survived deep in the bones of Arakis and his family. It was as if he kept it alive all these years to pay penance for bringing it to Egypt so many years ago. Thoth has blessed us and it, guiding our hands to the throats of our enemies."

"Well, neither one of us has it - so too bad for you," Jack said, taking Wendy's arm and pulling her away. "Looks like the 'ole plan didn't work."

Raul smiled at them. "I will admit there have been some-" Raul paused, scratching his head. "-mishaps I would say."

"Yeah, like knowing your dig site was full of shit," Jack said.

"Well, yes that is some of it. I fear my formal leader was a bit of a romantic in his ways. You see he wanted you to get the curse down there in the caves of Arakis. There where the priest was buried with his family. My leader had romantic ideas. He was educated in the States and went to college for literary studies. It seems some of it took hold of him." Raul shrugged. "That does not matter any longer as he was killed in the plane crash you all saw. It was very clever to act as victims to get to the city and away from us. But the time has come for no more games. You will bring the curse to the West. I cannot rely on Dr. Edwards out there to infect you and to leave enough of you to make it back home. Therefore, we have taken some samples from the dead and dying ones on our way here." Raul reached behind the curtain and came back with two large needles. He smiled as he prepared them. Each was filled with a dark liquid. Suddenly, lights started to flicker.

Raul just chuckled. Jack could see the silhouettes of the two soldiers on the other side of the curtain. On the television, he was able to make out the woman explaining the traffic jams that the terrorist's attack on the hospital were creating. Jack thought about how people could just be going about their day when they were being threatened with something that could end Western civilization as we know it. Perhaps all civilization. He had to think of something … and fast! He looked at the ground. He saw the light from the window flash on the floor. On it was a laundry bag with a sticker. The first part was in Egyptian and the second in English. It read: All Hospital Laundry will be kept in the Basement for Pickup. This will include all operational suits and equipment.

All suits. Jack thought. He turned towards the window with a plan formulating in his head. One small problem, however, he thought. He looked up at Raul who was now stepping towards Wendy. "I don't give a damn any more who brings it back. Just as long as it gets there." He lunged at Wendy, but Wendy moved around the bed too fast. Raul growled at the men behind the curtain, but got no response. Jack could see from the light behind the curtain that the two who were there had left. Raul shot a nasty look as Wendy headed for the curtain. His foot slipped on the way, and he nearly fell to the ground. This seemed to make him even angrier. He stood up straight as if regaining his composure when he looked down at what he had tripped on. Jack and Wendy also now saw what it was. Blood spilled out from the other side if the curtain. They watched as a shadow materialized from the floor and then rose over Raul's head, still behind the curtain. Raul slowly reached for his gun. Jack knew this was his one chance to get out. He quietly stepped behind Raul.

"HEY, DAD!" he yelled and kicked Raul into the curtain. The thing behind it let out a cry of rage. The curtain came down on Raul, leaving the hulking figure of the cursed one. It ripped at the curtain viciously. The light-colored curtain turned red as it ripped away. The cursed one snapped down on Raul's neck and, between chewing and biting, his head came off. Suddenly, the window burst apart and two smoking bombs were in the room with them. The cursed one growled at the smoking cylinder and then turned and left, running down the hall on all fours, sneezing. Jack watched it go with Raul's eyes watching from

228

the monster's mouth. He was sure Raul was watching him with pure hate even with his head detached from his body.

When he looked back, Wendy was already coughing and falling to her knees. He sucked in some air and picked her up. At first, she resisted, but when she realized it was him she let him take her. He didn't know which way he was running as the smoke was starting to fill up everywhere. He passed a door and before he realized what was written above it, he was several paces beyond. *Stairs!* He stopped so quickly he almost dropped Wendy on the ground. "What is it?" she asked, looking around for danger. "I saw a sign for the stairs," he explained.

"What then?" Wendy asked, standing on her own now.

"I gotta plan," Jack said, grabbing her hand and feeling for the door handle in the smoke. He found it and it was unlocked. He opened it and they went inside fast. Inside, there was no smoke and they breathed, trying to stop coughing from the burning in their throats.

"What's next?" Wendy asked, getting control of her coughing fit. Jack liked the way she was trusting him and not questioning his every move as she had in the past.

"Hey, you guys down there?" Marty's voice called out to them from above. They froze, not able to move. "Ah, come on you two. You forget about your 'ole bud Marty already?" Jack could tell he was having trouble speaking now. "You alright, Mart?" As soon as he asked, Wendy slapped him hard in the chest. He knew he shouldn't have responded but … but it was Marty. Or at least he hoped it was.

229

"Hey, I was thinking, Jack."

"Yeah." Jack ansered back, still hiding out of view.

"Well at least let me see ya, big guy. I mean this could be our last face-to-face time, dude."

Jack slowly moved toward the railing, cautiously peering up. Wendy grabbed his arm, but Jack knew he had to do this. He leaned over the railing slightly and slowly tilted his head. Marty was several stairwells up from them. He leaned over the railing, smiling, his mouth full of sharp teeth. His face was black now with patches of fur around it. The only thing that was still Marty was a few dreadlocks hanging down his face as he bobbed his head, smiling at him. "What do you think of the new look, man?" Marty asked, spinning around. Jack couldn't be sure from where he was, but it also looked like Marty was several feet taller now. "What you going to do, Mart?"

"Hey, hey … what happened to 'we're gonna save you, buddy' speeches? Have we already crossed that bridge, buddy?"

"Marty … I'm so-"

"Oh, save the water works, Jackie boy," Marty laughed. It sounded more like choking. "You see buddy, I have a new deal for ya. You listening?"

"Yes, Mart."

"Good, because here it goes. You remember that cute little blond chick you are hiding down there?" Marty stuck out his now-elongated nose and sniffed the air. "Oh, you dirty boy!" he laughed. "You two have been making good use of your time, I see … or I mean smell. Well, any-who, here it is. The plan goes like this. I come down there and rip your sex toy open and eat her guts. I do so like eating the guts, Jack. Ain't that weird? I mean … me? A guy who couldn't even eat seafood because of the way it looked. Now I like warm steamy guts!" He laughed and then stopped suddenly, putting his nose over the railing again. He snorted like a dog and then growled deeply. "New plan," Marty said, disappearing from the railing. "That bastard doesn't get to have you! You're mine … MINE!"

Jack grabbed Wendy's arm and they started running down the stairs. Suddenly there was a boom. Jack risked a look up the stairs. He saw a large head come over the railing further up. Then he saw Marty's slightly smaller head look up at it. Marty growled and the larger one snarled back. Marty looked back down at Jack. "I told ya your dad never liked me. You think it's the hair?" He laughed and sprang away like an animal. Jack looked up again, but the bigger one was gone as well. "You're on your own sparky. Eat ya later!" Marty yelled from somewhere and then Jack heard a door slamming shut.

"The big one is coming!" Jack whispered frantically into Wendy's ear. She didn't need coaxing and they ran down the stairs two and three at a time. They heard the rumbling behind them as the cursed one chased them.

231

"The basement!" Jack said.

"Then what?" Wendy asked, nearly missing a step and falling.

"I'll think of something," Jack said, a little less confident.

The stairs ended and Jack pulled the handle to the door leading to the basement. He knew if that handle did not twist, they were dead. Jack's heart turned to ice as he felt the doorknob start to stick, but to his elation it kept going and he threw open the door. Wendy went first and he followed. They were about to step through as a dark shape hit the wall opposite them, growling savagely. It had lost its footing in its haste and fallen. Jack stepped in and pushed the lock on the handle of the door. He couldn't help thinking how insignificant the lock seemed when it was the only thing keeping the monster away from them -- the only thing that was allowing them to not be ripped to pieces.

"Come on!" Wendy called to him. "What ARE YOU doing?" she yelled. Jack realized he had been staring. Something hit the door hard and Jack fell backward on his ass, staring again at the door as he saw the top half bending away from the frame.

"JACK!" Wendy screamed.

Jack shook his head and headed in the direction Wendy was calling. He went through some double doors and saw she was standing by what looked like a large garage door. She was peeking through a crack, looking at something on the other side.

"Is it through yet?" she asked, without looking at him.

"It will be in a second."

"Good."

"Good? How is that good? We got to get out of here!"

"There are men with guns just outside this door," Wendy said, finally turning to look at him. "Stand by the button over there," she said, pointing. "When it's just about on me, push the button. And Jack-"

"Are you fucking nuts?" Jack asked her wide eyed.

"Don't hit it again until it's all the way open."

"You've lost your damn-" They heard the door slam open. They then heard the long intake of breath that meant it was sniffing the air for them. Jack looked over and saw the button. He ran for it just as he heard the heavy footfalls behind him. He turned with his hand ready to push it. The monster was in the room. It stood at its full height. It was looking remarkably better, he thought. There was hair again where there had only been dead charred skin. It turned slowly towards Jack, and he saw that it still had one white dead eye. It turned away towards Wendy again as if confused about who to eat first.

"Hey dad." Jack called to it. The beast's head snapped towards him with a growl. "You remember how you missed almost every Christmas ... and every other holiday for that matter?"

"Jack what are you doing?" Wendy asked in a low, angry tone.

"Well, I just want to say that was a real dick move, you know. I guess what I'm getting at … is you're a dick." Jack shrugged. "A big hairy burned up grotesque DICK!"

"Jack!"

The cursed one charged. "Use the chain!" Jack yelled. "It opens it manually!"

Jack crouched down and closed his eyes. He felt the hot breath in his ear. Then all he heard was shooting. A lot of shooting … and some yelling. He opened his eyes and he saw men in military gear pouring into the room with guns in their hands. They ran through the way he and Wendy had come. It was dark and he didn't think they saw him crouching there. He looked around and saw Wendy standing with her back against a wall and her hands above her head. She was pleading with a man that had a gun pointed at her chest. Jack saw a wrench near his foot. He picked it up and threw it at the soldier's head. It clanged noisily off the wall, far from where Wendy and the soldier were. They both looked at him, confused by what he was trying to hit. Wendy took the opportunity and kicked the soldier in the groin, and he went down.

"What now?" she asked.

"This way!" Jack waved to her. The soldier swore at her in Egytian as she passed. Jack headed for a door further in. He opened the door. He looked around inside quickly and pulled Wendy with him. "This is what I was looking for."

"The plan?"

234

"Yeah, the plan."

"You plan to act the idiot hero again?" Wendy asked, her eyes wide and enraged.

"Hey, I had some father-son issues to resolve." He shrugged. Wendy stared at him and he saw tears running down her cheeks. "Hey, we're going to get out-"

"Listen asshole," Wendy said, cutting him off. "I like you." She wiped a hand under her nose. "You just stay alive. That's all." Jack came up to her and, at first, she started to push him away. As he persisted, she put her arms around him and kissed him. "*You're* the dick," she said under her breath.

"Like father like-"

"Finish that and I'll make you wish you were that soldier."

"Ok, so let's get to work then."

Jack went from box to box looking inside. Each time he didn't find what he was looking for he swore. Finally, at the end of a row of boxes he found it. "YES!" he elated.

"Are you going to tell me what you're looking for or what?"

"Yes, these." Jack held up a Bio-suit. The Plexiglas helmet flopped forward as he presented it to Wendy for viewing.

"What do we do with that?"

"We get the hell out of here!"

CHAPTER 22
ESCAPE FROM HELL

The large door leading outside was closed again. Jack and Wendy stood by it looking out the small cracks. They could see clouds of smoke outside and soldiers walking through waving their guns back and forth. Several times, they saw flashes in the smoke and heard the gunshots. They watched as the men in the suits came and blasted their flamethrowers, giving off billowing smoke.

"They're still shooting everyone," Wendy said matter of factly.

"The people in the hospital are using the smoke to try to escape," Jack answered.

"Isn't that our plan?"

"No," Jack said, looking at her. "We are using the smoke to confuse them, not hide." He reached up and put the flimsy hood over her head. All the time, he searched the back of the room for any movement. He had no idea if his now furry father was still alive. And that was only half of their problems with the soldiers wanting to shoot them ... and of course fry them like marshmallows. Jack zipped the hood in place. He looked up and saw Wendy's blue eyes looking at him through the hood.

"You alright?" he asked her, thinking she looked funny with the hood flopping over to one side as she peered through the plastic.

"You ever think about having a family?" she asked.

237

"I don't know," Jack answered seriously. "I think if I found the right woman to have them with, I guess I would. I tell ya one thing though, I won't be a father like mine." He watched as Wendy smiled at him.

"What?" he asked, confused.

"Nothing, just thinking is all."

"You think we should get married and have a bunch of children or something --perhaps a house in the country with a picket fence?"

"Would that be so terrible?" she asked, cocking her head. The flopping hood nearly bent in half. Jack started to laugh, and Wendy took offence.

"Don't be an asshole!"

"No-no it's just that your-"

"I know what it is," she said, pushing him away. "Let's do this." Jack groaned and put his own hood on. He glanced back and saw Marty standing in the shadows staring back at him. Jack felt goosebumps run up his spine. Marty's skin was completely black, and he almost missed him standing there quietly. Jack noticed he was leaning to one side. He looked down and saw that one of Marty's legs was bent awkwardly and ended as a canine foot would. His shirt was nearly ripped off and hung around his now dark muscled skin. Patches of fur covered him. One ear stood above his head, and it twitched as he watched. His yellow eyes stared back at him intently. For a second, he thought he saw the old Marty

238

in those yellow eyes and then they narrowed with anger. Jack knew his friend had slipped away. His heart felt as cold as ice.

"We got to go," Jack said inside his hood to Wendy.

"What?" Wendy asked, following his eyes. "What's there?"

"Marty was just there."

"Are you sure?"

"I'm sure." Jack felt guilt grip him. "He's gone."

"Yeah, I don't see him."

"No." Jack turned "I think I just saw the last of him ... fade away. He is only the cursed one now."

"Oh, Jack I'm so-"

"Forget it," he interrupted. He looked around the room and ran to a wall. He pulled a fire extinguisher from its place. "There." He pointed. "Grab that one over there."

Wendy did as she was told, the whole time looking over at the place where Jack had said he had seen Marty. Her nerves were on edge, and she nearly fell over when she pulled and the extinguisher came free easily. She swore and started readjusting the hood. "You sure this is going to work? I mean, these look nothing like the suits those guys are wearing."

"We just have to make them believe we're not one of the hospital people. We just need a few minutes to slip away past the soldiers … that's all."

"So, they shoot fire and we're carrying extinguishers?"

"As I have already said … we need just a couple of minutes."

"Fine. Let's do it then."

Jack looked back to where Marty had been one more time and put his hand on the chain of the big door. He saw nothing there but darkness. Something caught his eye before he looked away, and he concentrated, looking into the darkness.

"What is it?" Wendy asked.

Jack put a finger near his lips the best he could with the hood of the bio suit up. There it was again. Something moved. It seemed to have come from the ceiling and landed on the floor. There was an overhang blocking his view of the ceiling so he squinted at the floor. He saw what looked like a pool of water gathering there. Jack looked up again and he saw a clawed hand grip the overhang. He watched as the cursed one tipped his big head below the overhang and looked at them. It snarled before dropping to the ground.

"OPEN THE DOOR!" Wendy yelled.

Jack pulled the chain and the door started to open. "Stand on the side." he pointed, "so they don't shoot you trying to get to that thing!"

Wendy moved, still staring at the monster now stepping towards them. It seemed to be confused by the suits as it put its nose in the air trying to smell them.

As the door opened, smoke entered the room around their feet and went as high up as the door, making it to the top. Jack hoped the soldiers would see the cursed one right away and start shooting, but it seemed the smoke was too thick for them to see it.

"Come on!" Jack ran to Wendy and grabbed her hand. He plunged into the smoke and took a sharp turn away from the door. He felt the cursed one move by him rather then saw him. He was thankful for the mask as he would be choking already at this point.

"Which way?" Wendy whispered. They could hear gunshots and the crackling of fire. Jack followed the light of the fire not knowing what to expect. He moved slowly and kept low.

"Stay close," he whispered, hoping she could hear him through the hood. He could make out something burning on the ground. As he got closer, he saw the outstretched hand from the ground. It was burned and still sizzling with the flames that lazily ate the last of its victim's flesh. Jack and Wendy looked down at it. They could see that she was clutching something to her breast. As the smoke moved, they realized it was a small child.

"She was trying to protect her child," Wendy said, her face hidden inside her hood. "We are in hell. This is hell."

"Hey," Jack touched her arm. He felt her jump. "We're almost out, we're going to make it." Wendy turned to face him, and he saw her eyes were wide and terrified. "Hey, come on now. Don't give up-" That's when he heard the heavy breathing behind him. He realized the cursed one was right behind him. "You run," he said to Wendy without turning yet. "RUN!" He swung the fire extinguisher around, hoping to get in a lucky shot. Next thing he knew he was sliding across the hard pavement unable to breathe. It felt like he had been hit by a car. He slammed into something hard with his back and he closed his eyes, wondering if his back was broken. He heard Wendy scream and he forced his eyes open. He tried to stand and to his surprise everything worked. He limped through the smoke towards where he had heard her voice. He saw movement in the smoke and realized it was too small to be the cursed one. He ran towards it, hoping it was her.

Wendy stood still in the smoke. Her heart was beating so loud she thought it would give her away. She listened, but all she could hear was her own breath in her hood. She slowly spun around, looking for Jack in the smoke. She wished she had not dropped the damn fire extinguisher. As meager a weapon it was, it was still all she had. "Jack," she whispered, calling out into the smoke. She realized her voice could not carry beyond her hood and she frantically attacked the straps holding it on. She threw it off her head and was face to face with the cursed one standing in front of her. It looked into her eyes, and she could see the insanity that was inside it. She saw that there was no rational or even mundane thought going through its mind as it stared at her with nothing but blind simple lust for food. She couldn't help but think it was similar to the look in her calculus teacher's eyes.

She suddenly started to get angry from its hesitation and the way it stared. "What are you waiting for?" she said as it bounced up and down on its dog-like back legs. Each time it did she had to look up to follow its eyes. "Come on then!" she yelled at it. "-you gonna just stand there and breathe on me or what!" The cursed one blasted an angry growl in her face and spread its large, clawed arms from side to side as if ready to strike at any moment … but it didn't. Wendy wiped the slobber from her face with her gloved hand. "Well-" she spat on the ground and the cursed one watched the spot on the ground, sniffing. "If that's it then I'll be-" It wrapped its claws around Wendy's shoulders and lifted her into the air. Wendy closed her eyes and held her breath. The cursed one pressed its nose against her neck and face. Even though not breathing, Wendy got the odor of rotting flesh and nearly vomited. She felt the hot tongue touch her face. The smell from it was too much and she opened her eyes and vomited in its face. The cursed one dropped her to the ground, and she fell over, trying to control her retching. She was able to see it wipe the vomit from its face and smell its fingers. It seemed to find something in it that made it angry, and it screamed down at her with rage. Wendy thought it almost sounded more like disappointment than anger.

Jack saw her on the ground with the cursed one looking down at her. "NO!" He ran through the smoke towards them, striking the cursed one on the back with the extinguisher. It moved away from Wendy but did not leave. Jack pulled the pin of the extinguisher and released the contents into the monster's face. It screamed with fury. As he eased off the contents of it, he saw that it was gone. He turned back to Wendy and saw that she was surrounded by soldiers. Many had their guns pointed at her, but most were looking at them confused. Their bio-suits were working as subterfuge but not for long. Jack dropped the extinguisher and started waving them away from Wendy. When he got closer, he took her hand and got ready to run. One of the soldiers must have sensed they were up to something and started yelling and pointing his gun. Another walked up to Wendy and roughly grabbed her arm. Wendy had an image of the cursed one grabbing her again and yelled. She put a hand on his uniform and pushed. The soldier was lifted into the air and disappeared into the smoke. Jack had no time to try to understand it. When he looked back at the soldiers to see what they would do next, one of them was pulled into the thick smoke behind them. Seconds later, the soldiers facing them were soaked in blood that came from the smoke. They turned to face where it had come from.

Next it came from the side and took a soldier's arm with it before disappearing again. The man screamed as he fell to his knees, trying to keep his blood from running out. One of the men called on a walkie talkie and fire all around them lit up. The one who had made the call shot two times in the air as an apparent signal. Two men in suits showed up with torches in their hands and gas tanks on their backs. The men were back-to-back and searched the smoke for movement, blasting their torches when they thought they saw something. Just as it seemed things were slowing down, one of the men with a torch screamed and was pulled face first into the smoke where his screams were suddenly silenced. The last man with the torch came in closer to them. Jack could see his eyes behind his hood. He was terrified and his flames were blasting erratically and coming far too close for comfort. They all started lining up to be right behind him so as not to get burned. There was a flash of fur in front of them. Everyone held their breath waiting for the torch to go off. When nothing happened, they started mumbling and then the soldier who had originally called for backup stepped around and gently touched the man's shoulder. As soon as he was touched, the man and the torch fell backwards. They saw that his face and a good part of his head were now missing. As he hit the ground, the torch shot out fire and the soldier went up in flames. He screamed and ran into the smoke, waving his arms above his head as he burned.

A gentle breeze came in and moved the smoke. Jack saw over his shoulder that the cursed one had another soldier in the air, and it was eating his midsection as the man fought to get free. He knew the thing was picking them off one at a time. He had to try something. He decided to take the flame thrower. He bent over to start taking it off the dead man when he looked up. The smoke shifted and there was Marty again. He was close to the ground and eating from one of the dead hidden almost completely by the smoke. He looked back at Jack with blood dripping from his mouth. Jack sped up the pace at freeing the pack and torch. Someone yelled to him, but he ignored it, trying to get the gas tanks loose. Then someone grabbed his suit, and he was pulled to a standing position to now face the soldiers. They yelled at him in what he assumed was Egyptian. Jack shook his head. He looked around for Wendy but couldn't see her. That worried him. He tried to leave, but two soldiers grabbed him and wouldn't let go. Then there was nothing but fur and blood. He knew the cursed one was attacking, but it was so fast and violent that he couldn't tell where it was coming from. The men tried to fight back; each was being silenced by a splash of blood. Jack fell to the ground. Then he felt himself being lifted into the air. He could see the men being ripped apart as he fell back to the ground. He put his hands behind him to sit up and felt something cold and hard. When he looked, he saw that it was one of the soldier's rifles. He grabbed for it. He looked back to the horrific scene of the men being ripped apart. He spotted the dead man with the gas tanks on his side close to the soldiers. He was struck with a dilemma. If he were to shoot the gas tanks, he would most likely be killing the cursed one but would probably be killing some of the men as well.

"Shoot it," Wendy said, next to him.

"Where'd you-"

"SHOOT IT!" she yelled at him. Jack took aim and shot. He missed. The cursed one stopped its frenzied attack and turned in his direction. It crouched and growled deep in its throat. Jack took aim again. He held his breath and pulled the trigger. Everything around them burst into flames. Jack slid across the pavement from the blast. He felt things falling all around him. He felt like he was suddenly deaf. When he opened his eyes, he saw the cursed one's head, which included an ear and an eye. Jack kicked it away frantically. His ears were ringing. He looked around for Wendy and saw her standing beside him with her hood still down.

"Hey-" he started but was stopped by a coughing fit. "-put the hood on." Wendy shook her head at him. "The hood," Jack yelled, thinking she couldn't hear him. He slowly got to his feet.

"You're on your own, Jack." He shook his head and she yelled it so he could hear.

"What are you talking about?"

"I'm one of them now, Jack. I'm one of the cursed ones."

"Don't be ridiculous, Wendy. You're just scared. Come on, let's go." Jack came forward and reached out his hand. As he did, a soldier ran up to Wendy and pointed a gun at her. Wendy moved faster than Jack could have imagined. She grabbed the man by the collar and trousers and threw him. The young soldier screamed as he flew up and into the smoke. Jack watched the way the smoke parted and left a trail where the soldier had sailed away through the air.

"Oh, no ... not you," Jack said, turning back, shaking his head, and feeling the tears swell in his eyes. He pulled the hood from his head. "I won't leave you. You can't..." He ran to her. Wendy extended her hands for him not to come any closer. "Stay away!" she yelled at him.

Jack stopped, now weeping freely. "I can't do it alone ... I won't!"

"Jack ... you must."

"Not without you!"

"Wendy is gone. I'm gone," Wendy said, now wiping her own tears away. "You can make it out, Jack." She started to backup into the smoke. "You find that home with the picket fence." She cocked her head sideways and let the tears flow as she backed away.

"NO!" Jack yelled. He felt hands on him now as the soldiers grabbed him. "NOT WITHOUT YOU!" He watched as Wendy put her face in her hands and turned to run into the smoke. The soldiers started firing at her. Jack went into a rage and fought to get free but there were too many. Some started beating him and he fell to his knees, covering his head. "Get off of me!" he yelled, throwing punches from his knees. Then he felt the cool metal of a pistol pressed against his head. He stopped fighting and waited for the darkness. For peace. For death. He had never felt as tired as right at that moment. He was done and didn't want to fight any longer. His best friend and now the girl he very well might be in love with was gone. He just wanted the pain to stop. He had no idea how long he knelt there waiting. When nothing happened, he slowly opened his eyes. And there was no one around him. There was some gunfire, but it was far off. He wondered if he was already dead. He looked down and on the ground in front of him was his father's journal with a soldier's pistol in the middle of it. He took the gun and read what was written on the page.

It read: "Think of me some time. Please remember me as I was - not what I am to become. I love you, W."

Jack sighed and took the journal and gun. He stood and reached behind him to pull the hood back on. He saw the flashing lights through the smoke, took another quick look around, and ran. He ran as fast as he could. Several times, he jumped over still smouldering bodies, but he didn't stop. At times, he passed soldiers and they glanced at him curiously but the suit was working. At times he looked over and thought something was keeping pace with him in the smoke. A breeze washed over him, and he saw Marty running with him now on all fours a short distance away. His clothes were tattered and his skin black. He still had some recognizable facial features, but it was really the few remaining dreadlocks that let Jack know that it was his best friend running with him like an animal. He decided to concentrate on what was in front of him and not the remains of his friend. He saw a line of military vehicles through the smoke in front of him. The soldiers also saw him coming and yelled out warnings. When he didn't listen to them, they fired at him. He heard the bullets ricochet all around him. He turned off thinking he should go deeper into the smoke. As he turned, nearly tripping on the wet pavement, he heard something crash into the vehicles and then the men yelling and shooting. He knew Marty was on them. He decided to use the distraction to his advantage and turned once more towards them. There were concrete barriers blocking off the hospital. He saw the men were now busy fending off Marty, so he ran by them and past the vehicles. He nearly ran straight into more soldiers. He pointed to where Marty was with the others and acted in what he would think someone of authority might and waved them towards the fight. They ran towards them enthusiastically. Jack ran on.

Past the soldiers, he could see policemen with guns at the ready. He knew there was no getting around them. He heard a boom in the sky and looked up. Fighter jets flew overhead. He suddenly had a bad feeling that if he didn't get out of there soon, he never would. Not far from the hospital was a dark alley. He ran there and saw what seemed to be an abandoned bicycle on the ground. No doubt someone was either frightened off or snatched up. He heard screeching tires and peeked around the building to see the police cars leaving. They were leaving very fast. He decided he too would leave the way they were going. He got on the bike and followed as fast as he could. He looked behind him and stopped. Marty stood down the street. He went again on all fours and ran towards him.

Come on, Mart. Gimme a break!

Jack put everything he had into the pedals. He felt like he was going fast. The buildings around him were flying past him. He kept peering left and right for obstacles and thought it strange that there were no people. He risked a quick look behind him and saw Marty not far away from him. He got a new rush of energy and put it into his legs. He quickly looked again and was sure Marty was catching up with him. Jack was pedaling so hard that he was nearly catching up with the last of the police cars as they fled from the hospital. They were getting jammed up.

He passed one of them and saw the police officer give him a stunned look as he flew by. Jack weaved in and out as cars slowed trying to get on a freeway. He looked back again and saw Marty leaping from car to car trying to get to catch up with him. For a short instant, Jack wondered if Marty had somehow won over the transformation and was trying to catch up with him to let him know that they could still go home

… together. Maybe, just maybe, Marty was alright, and things could go back as they were.

Jack remembered the look in Marty's eyes in the hospital … the way he could see his best friend slipping away from him. Not in a way that was sad as someone died in a hospital bed, but in a way that went from good to evil … in an instant. As if the goodness just ran out of him like the last drops of blood and all that was left was the darkness of a cursed one. Jack did not want to turn and look again for he knew he would just see the darkness in those yellow eyes. He resigned himself to pushing the pedals as hard as he could trying to see through the hot tears of guilt that now ran freely down his face.

Not far ahead on the highway's ramp was a police officer on a motorcycle. Jack rode his bicycle close to him and jumped off. The policeman stopped as he approached. As the police officer reached for his gun, Jack hit him hard in the face. His knuckles burned from it. The officer fell over sideways, and Jack grabbed the motorcycle before it tipped over. His only experience with a motorcycle was a mini-bike that he had as a kid. His last memory of that was losing control and hitting a stop sign at the end of his street. For months, his wrist was bandaged because of that mini-bike. He put it in what he hoped was first gear and hit the gas. He nearly flew off as it sped forward. He felt a mixture of guilt and elation as he saw Marty in the mirror tearing the policeman apart. Marty didn't take long though and Jack could see he was once again after him. He wove in and out of the police cars hoping the freeway was clear. He heard the jets flying over his head again but this time they seemed almost close enough that he could touch them. He instinctively crouched down and nearly hit the back of one of the police cars. Then there was an impossibly bright light behind him. He looked in his mirror, but everything was too bright to make anything out. Then the light was followed by an explosion. He felt himself being lifted off the motorcycle. He tried to hang on to the handlebars, but the force was too great, and he was thrown into the back windshield of the police car he had almost run into. He smelled cheap vinyl seats, sweat, and cheap air freshener ... then there was only darkness.

He dreamed he was back at school and he and Marty were sitting around watching a nature show on The Learning Channel. Marty was getting high and explaining everything about the African Killer Bee before the announcer would say it. He always seemed to know the most obscure things. They had finished off a large pepperoni and sausage pizza and the better half of a box of beer. They sat on their couch, stuffed, happy, and safe. Marty was wearing the same 'ole white poncho and nearly disintegrated jeans. He turned to Jack and let out the smoke like a dragon and laughed, then coughed.

"You're an ass," Jack said to him, shaking his head and laughing.

Then the front door opened, and Michelle walked in. Jack felt the familiar anger at her lack of respect by not even knocking any more. He hated her and knew she was just using Marty for a place to stay. She walked in but then stopped suddenly with her back to them. She tilted her head as if smelling something she didn't like in the apartment.

"There's some threemonths-old meatloaf in the fridge if you're hungry," he said, rolling his eyes at her back.

"Come on, man," Marty pleaded with Jack. "All we need is love," he sang in a perfect John Lennon impersonation. Michelle's head snapped down and turned slightly towards them. "You alright, honey?" Marty asked with genuine concern in his voice. Michelle turned towards them slowly. As she did, they noticed the glowing yellow eyes. Her lips curled up revealing sharp pointy teeth. She looked directly at Jack and leapt into the air straight for Jack's throat. He screamed and threw out his arms.

His eyes opened and he realized he was in a room. As much as it hurt, he turned his head. He saw medical instruments that let him know that he was in a hospital.

Oh, God! Not the hospital!

He panicked and tried to sit up. His head swam and everything faded in and out in tunnel vision. Stars appeared in front of him, and he felt himself fall back down. He could feel the sheets as he gripped them, trying to stay conscious. He took a deep breath, closing his eyes. In a few seconds he felt slightly better. He opened his eyes again and this time looked around as best he could without sitting up.

"It is best if you stay calm, Mr. Edwards," a deep voice said close to where he lay.

"Who-" It was all he could get out as his throat was so dry he couldn't speak another word.

"My name is not important," the voice said.

Jack suddenly had what looked like suit pants in his view. The man sat in a chair across from him. He could tell he was a Middle Eastern man. He had the demeanor of someone important.

"You are safe," he said.

"-am I?"

"Safe." The man pulled something out of his breast pocket and placed it on the night stand close to him. "Go home, Jack. All is arranged."

"What have you done to me?"

"You are as you were when you entered my country."

Jack thought it weird the way he said *my country*. As if he owned it all.

"I did try to end this," the man said, sounding sincerely remorseful. "I knew they were working on something… I had no idea what they had planned." He leaned forward and wiped his face with a handkerchief. "We have many people here that have hearts full of pain. They have unfortunately let their pain drain their hearts and fill with hate. That hate has led them to places-" The man stopped looking at the ceiling as if the words wounded him deeply. "-led them to places we have been before. History repeats itself, they say. Go home, Jack. Forget what you have seen here."

"Forget it!" Jack sat up again. This time he was able to stay that way. "I have lost my best friend and..." He paused as the image of Wendy came to him. "I have lost a lot in this forsaken place."

"Many have lost, Mr. Edwards. Right now, this and its surrounding lands are a place of loss. You have your life, and even though that does not seem like much right now. it is what you have. Take that and count yourself one of the lucky ones. Those in the hospital are not so lucky."

"It is gone ... the whole hospital?"

The man got up and walked to the door. Before opening it, he paused. "Terrorists have attacked the Cairo Hospital. None have survived. Many have died."

"Terrorists!" Jack yelled at him. "We know those jets weren't manned by terrorists."

"There were no jets. There were only terrorists trying to make a point by blowing up a hospital. That is all. Go home Jack."

"At least tell me you know what was really going on."

The man sighed. "Yes. I had tried to infiltrate the plan. I entered their lab and saw what ... things they were working with. We were about to close it down when ... this all happened. You have been involved in an unfortunate circumstance. Go home and try to forget all this."

"When the blast went off there was ... there was one after me."

"None survived."

"I did," Jack said, thinking he sensed something from the man by the way his shoulders dropped.

"There was a terrible automobile accident that killed your friend and assistant."

"She was no assistant," Jack shot back at him angrily.

"Call it what you will. They have died in a terrible accident. I am very sorry for your loss." With that, the man left the room. Jack looked at what was on the table and saw his passport and a plane ticket.

He was suddenly very angry, but then exhaustion hit him like a punch in the nose. He felt so tired he thought he could sleep for weeks. He closed his eyes, not caring if they ever opened again. From time to time, he would open them and he would see people looking down at him. His mind was so tired it seemed to refuse to wake up. He had flashes of getting on a plane. There were just flashes of faces and people trying to speak to him. He knew he should have worried that he was sick, but he just didn't care. He had a vague memory of being searched at the airport but was not sure if it was just a dream. There was a time that he smelled the scent that reminded him of the U.S. It was of fast food and cool sweet air. Someone pushed him through the airport, and it felt good seeing the other Americans. He was somehow home. But … it could be a dream. Perhaps this was just a cruel dream, and he was actually still in the back of the police car, unconscious and waiting for Marty to find him and feast on his entrails. He felt a pain in his arm, and he looked down and saw a needle being retracted from his flesh. He followed the needle to the sleeve of a feminine looking sleeve. Then darkness again. This time his father was there, and he didn't see him in the back of a classroom. His father was teaching the class about how to preserve artifacts found in the field. Jack looked around and saw a familiar face in the front row. It was Wendy. Her hair was shorter, and she looked younger … but it was her. He knew he was dreaming. He took another look around and noticed that all the people in the class were beautiful women. They all stared at his father like he was some religious prophet. Dr. Edwards lectured about maintaining the structure of an object as it was lifted from the ground. He bent down and acted like he was liberating a baby from the dirt. He cupped his hands and looked at them in a loving way. As if what was in there was the most important thing he had ever touched. Several of the women in the class sighed at his performance. Jack groaned and tried to get out of his seat but was unable to. He pulled but he was unable to move. He looked up and saw his father moving closer to Wendy as if to show her what was in his cupped hands. His father moved strangely, and Jack leaned over his desk. He saw Dr. Edwards was walking towards Wendy on canine legs. He leaned up and his father was almost to Wendy. As Dr. Edwards reached down, his eyes turned yellow. His mouth opened, revealing his long teeth. Wendy stared at Dr. Edwards' hands with her hands on her chest. Dr. Edwards slowly lowered his mouth over Wendy's head. Jack yelled but there was no sound. He looked at the others and they just looked at their beloved teacher as if he could do no wrong. Jack yelled in rage. The sounds that came out of his mouth sounded like the mixture of a man's scream and a wolf's lonesome howl. Just like what he would have heard in the desert night. He knew it sounded strange but now he couldn't stop. In the corner of his eye, he saw Dr. Edwards stop and snap his head towards him in rage. Long ears grew up on his head and then went flat as he bent over and snarled at him. The women in the room clapped, delighted. His father was now the full figure of a cursed one. He turned, pulled Wendy to his chest, and jumped across the room and out the window with a crash. Jack heard another sigh, this time in disappointment from the women. Jack got up free and ran to the window. He put a hand on the windowsill and jumped as a cursed one's claw was there. He jumped backwards but it came with him. He threw his arms in front of himself and saw that the claws were his own. He felt the cold chill and ... hunger.

He sat up and now he was back in his old bed in the apartment. There was no telling how long he was there. His head felt like it was as big as a boulder. His thoughts were jumbled and unclear. He only remembered getting up to go to the bathroom and then returning to sleep. Eating was not a problem as he was not hungry. A couple of times, he remembered searching the cabinets for food just because he thought he should eat, but when he found none he just went back to his bed. He was not sure if he was just tired or if he had been drugged. The fact was it didn't really matter to him anymore. In fact, nothing really mattered to him right now. He heard the house phone ringing every so often and he ignored it. He thought the ring had an unusually annoying tone to it and thought it must have been picked out by Michelle. A sudden pang of guilt hit him and sent him into a fetal position. He hugged himself as the tears came. His best friend was dead because of him. Maybe worse. And what of Wendy? He wished his head was not clearing. Now the images and understanding washed over him like a sea of blood. He let himself submerge into self-loathing and misery. He went so deep he knew there was a chance that he might never come back out. He rolled onto his back, feeling the springs of the old mattress underneath him. He stared up at the ceiling with tear-filled eyes. He let his mind wander numbly, staring. He could barely see with his eyelashes filled with tears. He squeezed his eyes and opened them. He looked at the ceiling, now able to see. He noticed that one part of the ceiling was particulary clean. Desperate to re-focus, he curiously looked to the other three corners. They were all covered in dust, and some had cobwebs … as he would have expected. Suddenly, he became even more curious and got up, looking around. He saw a vent in the ceiling near the clean part. Pieces of the rungs of the cover plate looked to be neatly cut away. He got a chair from outside the bedroom and looked inside. He could make out something shiny. A cold chill passed though him. He reached up and ripped the vent from the ceiling. It clanged to the floor loudly. Inside he found a small black camera. He was being watched. And there has been no telling for how long. Jack wanted to smash the face of the man who called himself Raul into pieces. If the man was not already dead, he would have taken pleasure in making him that way again. He stepped off the chair he was standing on and threw it across the room. The table it hit crumbled, and a book slid off into the middle of the room. It was his father's book. There was a sticky tab on it. It read. "When/if you make it back. Come see me. Dr. T. Usher. P.S. The book is to remind you that no matter how successful you have been … you will never be your father."

Blood rushed to his head as he gripped the note. His whole life, people had measured him against his father. Now that it was evident that dear Dr. Edwards was not the saint everyone thought he was, people were still comparing him.

I'm sick of taking this shit! Usher, did you know what they had planned for us? Did you know that he was putting your students in danger and that some could have even been killed? Did you even care? How much was mine and Marty's life worth that you sent us to that hellhole?

Jack held the note in his fist so hard his nails were drawing blood.

He knew! He knew and still he sent us. I have done nothing to the man, and he does this to me.

Jack felt a rage in him that he didn't even know that was possible. He had a focal point to put all the bad things that happened into.

-time to keep the appointment with the good Doctor Usher.

He opened two drawers before finding what he was looking for. Last year, Marty's parents had gotten him a cooking knife set. Nobody in the apartment knew what do with it … until now. He shoved his large knife in the backpack along with some of his books. He had no real plan in mind. He was just going to go to Dr. Usher's office … and kill him. Make him pay for what he did to Marty. For what happened to Wendy. Make him pay for what he had put them all through.

He ran the whole way to the building. It was cold, dark, and wet. He wore a dark red hoodie over his head as he opened the main door and took two stairs at a time towards Usher's office. There was a line of students waiting outside. He heard Usher yelling and the door opened. A young coed ran out crying. Jack heard Usher's sarcastic voice call out, "Next." Jack ran up and grabbed the pimpled-face boy in front and pulled him back. The boy started to resist, but looked into Jack's face and stepped away.

"Come on-come on … get in here already," Dr. Usher said from inside his office. Jack stepped in without putting down his hood. He gently closed the door and walked to the window.

"Yes-yes. What can I do for you?" Jack watched the reflection in the window as the pudgy man looked at his watch, pretending he had somewhere else to go. Most likely, the fat little man would be picking up porn at the local video rental store and jerking off in his mother's basement where he lives. He turned and looked at him from deep inside the hoodie. He felt bile coming to his throat.

He turned away and started drawing the curtains shut.

"Excuse me!" Dr. Usher said angrily. "I do not remember saying you could touch those." Usher got to the edge of his seat, but no further. "Can we just get this over with, already?"

"Yes, we can," Jack said, letting go of the string that pulled the curtains.

"Who are you?" Dr. Usher demanded. Jack just stared at him from the darkness of the corner of the room, the hood covering most of his face. "Oh, my god … is that you?" he asked, stretching his fat neck forward to see.

"Surprised?"

"No … I mean," Dr. Usher took a moment to compose himself. "So you're back. So what."

"I think we had a bargain," Jack said, pulling his backpack from his shoulder.

"I don't know what you are trying to accomplish with all these dramatics, but let me assure you it is not helping your position with this school, *Jack* Edwards."

Having his name said in that way was like shoving a handful of bamboo under his fingernails.

"Where's that drug addict little friend of yours?"

"Dead-" Jack paused, thinking. "If not dead … then mostly dead."

"What is mostly dead?" Jack could hear the man swallow nervously. "Listen boy, I have not the ti-" Before he could finish, Jack moved across the room so fast the curtains ruffled by the window. "Wendy's dead, too," Jack said, putting his hands on the desk.

"Who- who's Wendy?"

"Another friend. Another friend YOU HAVE KILLED!"

Dr. Usher sat up straight in his chair in defense. "Do not put your bad fortune on me, young man," he yelled back, red-faced. "Just because some stupid girl had the bad sense to accompany another Edw-" Before Dr. Usher could finish, Jack had the knife out and was slicing the air on its way to his throat. The knife cut through the flesh in the way the commercials had always promised. It didn't even bleed at first. But when Dr. Usher stood, the blood began to flow down into his already stained yellow short sleeve dress shirt. He grabbed at his throat with both hands, shock in his small pig-like eyes. Jack saw that he meant to run for the door. Dr. Usher stepped out but Jack was too fast. He plunged the steak knife twice more into the man's side. Dr. Usher was very fat and none of the wounds were bringing him down. Jack watched silently as the professor turned around and around in the small room, not knowing what to do as blood ran out of him from many wounds. He ran for the curtains and pulled. The rods snapped and they fell to the floor. If anyone were to pass by his window, which was unlikely on the third floor, they would have seen a very fat bald professor banging on a window as he bled to death. All the while, they would get glimpses of someone in a hooded sweatshirt moving up and down behind him, arm raising and falling over and over again. Each time, the professor's mouth opened and closed, pleading for it to stop.

Jack scrubbed at the blood on his hands in the faculty bathroom. He thought he should be feeling frightened and even repulsed by what he had done. The fact was that Jack was feeling better than he had in a long time. He knew the other students would probably be opening Usher's door about now, especially after the lame excuse he gave while opening

263

the door and running down the hall. He couldn't help but laugh. It must have looked like something from a horror movie walking out that door. He told the others that Dr. Usher had cut his finger on his broken coffee mug and that he was off to find a band aid. Jack started laughing so hard he had to press his back against the wall to hold himself up. He slid down, putting his hands on his knees. He thought they looked odd, stained as they were. He looked at them, flipping them over and over, studying them. Finally, he stood up and put them under the light. He scratched at a small patch of something black on his skin and he frantically saw the pieces fell away. He was so relieved he didn't even bother with the rest of it. He threw his sweatshirt in the garbage and walked out the door. He heard the screams as someone finally opened the dead doctor's door. Jack thought the doctor got off easy. He walked into the cool night, stopped by the steps, and took a deep breath. He smelled pizza in the air and suddenly he was famished. He decided to go find some food. He felt as if he hadn't eaten in weeks. The thought of pepperoni and sausage pizza consumed him. Jack was hungry.

CHAPTER 23
WEAPON

They watched from the dark room. They smoked cigarettes and talked lightly about what was sitting there in front of them.

"It is not right to have her showing herself like that," a Middle Eastern man in desert fatigues said with disgust in his voice but with something entirely different in his eyes.

"You go and cover her up." Another laughed.

"Shut your mouth!" The first threatened with a fist. "We are not here to see a naked woman. What is the point of this?" the man demanded.

"The point-" a man in the back started as he stood up from his chair. "-is that this pretty girl in there is probably the most dangerous thing on this planet right now."

"She doesn't seem too dangerous from where I'm looking."

The man in the suit moved forward and took her in. Wendy sat on a slab of cement. Her arm covered her breasts as she turned away from them. Her long blond hair fell like angel wings down her back. Her head was bent as if praying. She looked more like a beautiful Roman scultpture than a lethal biological weapon.

"Hey," the man slapped the glass. "It's your friend!" the man said, instigating her. Wendy opened a blue eye. "You still in there or has the beauty now become the beast?" He laughed.

There was a flash of movement so fast none could react. The sound of her hitting the glass echoed all around them. Now Wendy looked in at them, sizing each one up individually. Only this was no longer the beautiful sculpture. Now this was the horror of the transformation. Wendy's entire left side was black with tufts of fur. Her leg was that of a canine and it was being held back by the chain holding her. She ran her clawed hand down the glass as she stared in with her one blue and one yellow eye.

"This will not hold me forever," she whispered to them.

"It held the last one," the man in the suit said calmly, with hands behind his back.

"Seems to me he got out. I will get out too." Wendy licked the glass. "And I'm going to rip you open." She pressed her chest and stomach against the glass. She knew how these men were uncomfortable with her naked body and she wiggled seductively against the glass.

"No way!" one of the men said, getting up and walking out.

"Wait!" the man in the suit said, running after him "You don't have to use it, you just have to own it! It's much like nukes... WAIT!" The man held his arms out pleadingly as he left the room. "We have ways of suppressing the transformation."

266

Wendy watched as the door closed. As it did, she bent down and started scratching under the glass. Pieces of cement crumbled away. She looked through the glass with satisfaction as she wiggled a clawed nail on the other side now. "We'll be having that meeting real soon," she said, smiling with her long sharp teeth glistening in the fluorescent light.

CHAPTER 24

MARTY

"And in other news-" the beautiful dark-skinned woman news broadcaster said, looking at the cameras and reading off the teleprompter. "Egypt is being plagued with a series of wild dog attacks. Half eaten-" The broadcaster stopped, squinting at the teleprompter as if unsure if she was reading it right. Her ruby red lips went up showing off her perfectly veneered teeth. "-it seems wild dogs have been attacking and – consuming their victims. The UN has been called in to help the local police catch and destroy the animal or animals." She shook her head, letting her midnight black hair move, its first sign of life since the broadcast started. "Let us all hope they find and destroy these things quickly." She then smiled brightly. "And in other new…"

Five policemen slowly walked down the dark alley with shotguns in their hands. Their eyes jerked back and forth, looking for any movement. One of their radios squawked and the others gave him a dirty look. The man hurriedly turned it off. As he did, a drop of something wet hit his shoulder. He looked at the others and saw that they were already searching the alley again. Another drop fell and he slowly raised his head. He saw two yellow lights halfway up the building. As his eyes focused, he realized there was a single blond dreadlock hanging between the lights. He watched them blink once and then they seemed to get bigger followed by darkness beyond. That was the last thought the policeman ever had.

www.ingramcontent.com/pod-product-compliance
Lightning Source LLC
Chambersburg PA
CBHW061600170626
46811CB00001B/265